WEIRD HORROR MAGAZINE

SPRING 2023

ISSUE 6

EDITED BY
MICHAEL KELLY

UNDERTOW
PUBLICATIONS

WEIRD HORROR 6
Spring 2023

PUBLISHER
Undertow Publications
Pickering, Canada

EDITOR/LAYOUT
Michael Kelly

PROOFREADER
Carolyn Macdonell

OPINION
Simon Strantzas

COMMENTARY
Orrin Grey

BOOKS
Lysette Stevenson

COVER ART
Asya Yordanova

COVER DESIGN
Vince Haig

INTERIOR ART
Simut Roy

https://www.weirdhorrormagazine.com

CONTENTS

ON HORROR

SIMON STRANTZAS

HORROR'S MOUNT RUSHMORE

THE THREE MOST important Horror writers are Stephen King, Clive Barker, and Thomas Ligotti.

The first question you're going to ask is what do I mean by "important." In this case, I mean these three writers were important in shaping the Horror genre. More specifically, the American Horror genre.

There are really two Horror genres: the American genre and the British genre. All writers who write Horror (by which I mean work explicitly marketed as Horror) are working within the outlook of one of these two distinct genres. If the writing does not adhere to one of these the work is not Horror. It may be "horror" (i.e., stories of the malignant unexpected invading the expected) but it is not "Horror" as we understand it. Japan, for example, has a long history of ghosts and demons, but stories written about these myths don't necessary adhere to the rules of Horror. Horror, as it stands now, is a decidedly Western phenomenon. One forged by the American and British traditions.

What makes American Horror different from British Horror? Over-simply: in Britain, Horror is an established tradition that is part of Britain's history. Paganism, witchcraft, religious wars. Christmas ghosts. These things are not part of the New World, whether it's because America was too recently settled or because its settlers developed it as a puritanical state, and that puritanism is baked into American values. Horror, as a result, has not been welcomed into the fabric of American art in the way it has in Britain. In America, Horror is wholly ghettoized.

There's a second cultural reason: America's primary mythology is one of cowboy exploration. Of heading west to meet the challenges of the New World. Contrast this with the weight of Britain's established history. The people of the former applaud heroism, the latter perseverance. The former are self-assured, the latter are self-doubting. These fundamentally different perspectives created parallel genres of Horror.

To summarize it another way: had the Horror Boom not happened, I suspect there would be no significant market today for Horror in America; in Britain things might very well be as they are currently.

Back to those important American writers...

I start with Stephen King because, arguably, there was never a Horror Boom—there was Stephen King and then a litany of writers unsuccessfully sold by their publishers as his equal and successor. A whole genre built on an attempt to duplicate one writer's success. King may not have been the Primary Mover of American Horror literature, but he was and is its biggest and only star. There were no stars before him and it's doubtful there will be any after him. He is *sui generis*, and inarguably important.

So much of what we think of as American Horror comes from King's work. The small towns, the folksy people with secrets, the faint air of camp. King learned a lot of this from the California circle of writers who preceded him—the Bradburys and Mathesons and Ellisons—writers who wrote stories and books but also wrote television and film scripts. Even the Horror Boom began with the publication of three novels written by screenwriters and/or actors. The cinematic structure of Horror evokes an arguably simplified view of how it functions, and set the rules for everything that followed. Of all these writers, though, King was the one to really perfect it, and only after interjecting it with the sort of grotesque morality found in places like old EC Comics stories.

The genre worked on mining King's work—namely, the quaint small-town terrors that typified American Horror—for a good decade before something unexpected happened: a British writer decided to make the jump into the explosively popular Horror market and bring to it something contradictory. Something *perverse*. Clive Barker brought the taboo and transgressive to Horror on a wide scale. He brought sex. But not vanilla sex. Weird sex. Discomforting sex (at least, discomforting if you were used to the puritanical kind). During the 80s neon and leather and androgyny hit the zeitgeist and Barker was able to infuse Horror with this implied perversity and force the field to reconsider what Horror was capable of. Barker's work was an inflection point for the genre. Once Barker appeared, nothing could be the same.

The last of the important American Horror writers is Thomas Ligotti. Ligotti's European and philosophical influences set him apart from nearly every writer in the field at the time. Unlike King and Barker, though, Ligotti's importance isn't illustrated by his commercial success or by the genre's immediate reaction to him. Instead, his importance lies in the effect he had on writers that followed him nearly a decade later. I'd argue that all post-millennium Horror writers (i.e., who we sometimes call Weird Fiction writers) are working in conversation to Ligotti, whether in concert with his work or at odds with it. Every weird writer is either running to or running away from the ideas he introduced into the field. Without his work, we might still be living in a world where Horror was relegated to diminishing cycles of vampire and zombie retreads.

Those three writers remain the most important, most influential, even now. Were there other important writers? Of course. I'd point to the late Peter Straub as a prime example. Straub bridged the gap between the schlocky Horrors that followed King and the experimental literary fiction being written by folks that wouldn't be caught dead reading Horror stories. Straub showed us that you could still be narratively and structurally exciting while telling a genre story. Yet despite his importance, I'd argue he didn't have the same transformative effect on American Horror that King, Barker, and Ligotti had.

Who will be the next important Horror writer? We probably won't know until many years after they begin their career, but considering how the internet has deconstructed every monoculture we once had and has freed the individual from their gatekeepers, I suspect there won't ever be another writer as important as these three were—no one else will be allowed the opportunity to be as transformative. At least, not as an individual. I believe the future instead lies not with particular authors but with groups of authors. The rising minorities that were until now excluded but who, using new opportunities like the increasing popularity of micropublishing, will finally get their chance to rewrite the genre in their image.

GREY'S GROTESQUERIES

ORRIN GREY

INTELLIGENCE WHERE NONE SHOULD BE: THE HORROR OF INANIMATE OBJECTS

"THAT WAS his idea of nightmare: the knowledge of sly intelligence where none should be." In Brian Lumley's novel *Necroscope*, this is the end of a several-paragraph meditation on the things that terrified the book's villain during his boyhood, culminating in an account of a cricket "leprous grey from the sightlessness of its habitation" that jumped on him in his father's wine cellar.

"To him there was fear in a creaking tread on a dark landing; there was terror in the tapping of a twig on his bedroom window, when all the house was asleep; there was horror in the sudden squirm or hop of a toad, or the startled freezing of a cockroach when the light is switched on, and especially in its scurrying when it knows it is discovered."

These things scare him, it says, because he is still a child, he does not "understand words like bestial, sadistic, diabolic." But they scare us all, don't they? At least a bit. If not specifically the cockroach or the toad, that idea of intelligence where none should be. Who amongst us hasn't had the thought, before we crushed a spider or stepped on a bug, that its kin would know what we had done, and would come for us?

We can talk all day long about the uncanny valley and the like but this, ultimately, is at least a part of the fear at the heart of the trope of the sinister doll. A doll *looks* like something intelligent, but it should not be. It should be inert, just wood or plastic. The same goes for a corpse. We know that at one time it was a person, but now it is just rotting meat—and yet, we fear that it will move once again, that it thinks still.

For me, at least, few things work better than when a horror story can successfully show us fear in a handful of dust—can truly imbue the inanimate with threat, with malice, with that "intelligence where none should be." In many ways, the killer doll like Chucky from *Child's Play* or the walking dead of a zombie movie are the clumsiest form of this, and the one that perhaps speaks least to that primal fear.

Which is not to say that they aren't frightening, necessarily, but that their horror is more firmly rooted in other fears. The fear of the knife, the fear of contagion—fear for our own safety and bodily autonomy. For an inanimate object to strike that truly primal fear, it must remain inanimate, or nearly so. Perhaps moving only when it is unobserved, as with the Annabelle doll from the popular *Conjuring* series of films.

But the object need not be animate at all for that sense of a malign, implacable will to be conveyed. Look at the corpse in the "Drop of Water" segment of Mario Bava's classic anthology film *Black Sunday*, the old man's staring eye in Poe's "The Tell-Tale Heart," the red ball bouncing down the stairs in *The Changeling*, even the puzzle-box at the heart of Clive Barker's *Hellraiser* franchise.

One of the oddest examples I can think of allows the object to move while still remaining inanimate, imbuing it with a sinister impression of will without actually giving it intelligence. *The Monolith Monsters* is an unlikely 1957 take on the standard "big bug" movie of the '50s. Only, instead of atomically irradiated ants or alien invaders, the film's antagonists are rocks.

These rocks fall from space and lie inert on the desert floor unless and until they get wet. When that happens, they quickly grow into towering pillars of crystal that eventually become too heavy to hold themselves up, at which time they crash over, shattering into a million pieces that then all begin growing in their turn. In this way, the space rocks more closely resemble how some plants and fungi spread and propagate than they do your standard movie monster.

And yet, the rocks in *The Monolith Monsters* are legitimately chilling, much more so than many of the more ambulatory critters that infested drive-in moves of the 1950s. This is thanks partly to their inexorable approach, the way that the special effect of the growing crystals still looks impressive and somewhat inexplicable today, and their ability to stand in for any number of metaphors that you may want to apply to them—but it's also, I think, due to their very lack of intellect.

An intelligent creature can, theoretically, be reasoned with. Its motives can at least be understood and avoided. There's a reason, after all, why we transform the tropes of the slasher film into "rules" that we think we can follow to stay safe. A malign will backed by an alien intellect—or no intellect at all—is more impossible to suss out, and therefore all the more chilling.

I've averred before that this underpins one of the most haunting aspects of John Carpenter's *The Thing*. The creature in that film is obviously intelligent—capable, indeed, of interstellar flight in a highly advanced spacecraft, and even capable, potentially, of rebuilding a similar craft from scratch. When it takes over and replaces a person, it seemingly knows everything that they knew and, until it is discovered, it converses as them unerringly, so perfectly that no one can detect the replacement.

Despite this, when the creature is, eventually, found out, such communication immediately ceases. The eponymous Thing makes no effort to explain itself, to sway those it encounters to its way of thinking, or even convince them to let it go in peace in exchange for it doing the same for them. Once it has been revealed, it slays or is slain. It obviously *can* communicate, it clearly *could* explain its motives, but it chooses not to.

For the rocks in *The Monolith Monsters*, there isn't even that. No ability to communicate and, indeed, nothing *to* communicate if there were. They have no actual intelligence, so far as we know, just the illusion of it—which, it turns out, is scary enough.

FARROW

RORY SAY

HE ENTERED their lives only after he'd ruined them. It must have seemed like a sensible idea. Certainly it was unplanned, just as the ruining had gone unplanned. These sorts of things simply happened in this sort of world, or so he'd come to reason. He was not one to question ideas presenting themselves as sensible.

Which is why when he came upon the house, he stopped outside. He'd been walking hollow, his thoughts funnelled deep into a husk of himself. Even the memory of what brought him here had gone, or partly gone, evaporated in the briny, stinking air. He realized this only after he'd stood looking at the house for a while, a beige raised bungalow. For some reason he expected to be met out front by the man who lived here, on the balding white lawn perhaps, but no one showed up. All the lights were out, too. Only his reflection looked back, hesitating in the wide picture window.

A dog slunk by behind him. He turned and watched as it paused, raised a hind leg, and pissed for a long while on the base of a birch, beholding him intently as it did so. He had to stand there and wait for it to stop, but it didn't stop and eventually seemed as if it never would. There was no owner in sight.

"You here to look at the suite?"

He turned back to the house and saw the man out front like he'd imagined, standing on the steps with his hands stuffed in the pockets of a cardigan.

"I'm sorry?"

"The basement suite."

He glanced again at the dog that was still there, darkening the birch's bright bark with its endless stream.

"My name's Sal," he said to the man.

They looked at each other.

"Private entrance is around the side," the man said. "I'll show you."

The handshake they shared was limp and without eye contact. The man failed to offer his name, which dismayed Sal because he'd forgotten it. He only remembered the boy's name, Seamus, who would be nine years old forever.

The suite was what he might have expected had he had the opportunity to expect anything: a sparsely furnished white-carpeted living room that gave on to the laminate floor of a somewhat sad kitchenette; the bedroom small and spare; the bathroom a bathroom. It took two minutes to see it all, maybe less, and afterwards Sal felt an awkward resistance to leave so soon.

He found himself asking questions that sounded plausible. Had there ever been a flood? Black mold or insects? What height was the ceiling?

The man came off as helpful but reticent in his responses, quietly eager to be somewhere else. He spoke softly, as though someone were asleep nearby, and the way he kept running his hands over the smooth dome of his bald head before plunging them in his pockets put Sal vaguely on edge.

"You live here alone?" Sal asked after they'd both fallen quiet.

His host apparently had to consider this. "No," he said, distracted. He'd begun gazing out the high basement window, the lawn's dead grass scraping the pane. Sal imagined him standing just like this long after he himself had gone, not moving or thinking, his eyes fixed to the window. The thought terrified him.

"I have a wife," the man added, "and we have a son."

"Of course," Sal said, nodding solemnly, unsure as to whether he was being confided in.

~

It rained hard on the day of the move. They had made no specific arrangements, or none that Sal could recall. He simply found the side door ajar when he arrived, rain soaking the carpet's edge, a single key waiting by the kitchenette sink.

He set to work piling boxes against one wall until he'd covered the window. Nobody came down to offer assistance, or even to make themselves known. From the outside, the house again appeared empty, unlived-in, an air of neglect to the washed-out walls and dim windows that made Sal lonesome for something his thoughts could not place. Even the suite itself looked seedier than he remembered from the viewing, as though much time had passed between then and now. The black mold he'd been assured wasn't there crept in at the ceiling's corners, while beneath his feet the carpet felt tattered in patches, frayed here and there as if by the claws of some animal.

Then there was the staircase beside the bedroom he hadn't noticed earlier, or if he had then he'd forgotten it was there. From time to time his curiosity led him up the steps to a door at the top, the white paint scratched and peeling. But whenever he reached the last step and prepared to knock or try the knob, he suddenly felt like a child on a dare, giddy with nerves that half paralyzed him. Once he put his ear to the frame and heard the sound of running water—a faucet left on and forgotten, perhaps—but by the time he descended the stairs and had taken another box from the diminishing mound of his life's posses-sions, he couldn't be sure that what he'd heard wasn't only rainwater spilling from a down-pipe outside. He would forget the door until the next time he noticed the stairs, until he built the courage to take one step followed by another.

~

At night he slept poorly. Parts of his body bothered him. Lying on his left, he became acutely aware of his own heartbeat, a dull thudding that seemed somehow separate from the rest of who he was. He began to visualize his heart as some trapped creature—some heart-sized *thing*

—throwing itself incessantly against the cage of his ribs, needing to get out. On his stomach it was worse, and on his back he felt it even though it wasn't there, a phantom pulse, and he had to resist the urge at all times to put a hand to his chest, afraid, presumably, he'd feel nothing at all.

So he lay curled on his right, always keeping to one half of the mattress with his back to the other half. He saw in his head the stairs outside his bedroom door that led to another door, the two lives above that had once been three. Or four. There had been a dog, he remembered. The boy on the bike had been chasing after some dog when he'd braked in front of Sal's truck. How had he forgotten the dog? After all, it was the dog that had startled him too badly to stop for the boy. Plus there'd been no lights, of course, because it had happened in Farrow, twenty miles away from anywhere if it could be said to be there at all —the ghost of a hamlet abandoned decades ago, harbouring only a few collapsed structures and the sharp reek of a rotting wharf.

Which was precisely what drew him in the first place. Finally he'd found somewhere that was his because it belonged to no one else. A week might pass without a soul in sight while he scoured the grounds, never finding much, and lived out of his truck. He relished the empty quiet, broken only by the surf and the cry of seabirds. He loved the salty air warm in his lungs, the clinging stink he could smell even now in his sleep.

But what kind of parents were they, letting their little boy go and play all by himself in a place like that, so far away and not even there? Or had they let him? Did they have any idea? He wondered this when he awoke over and over on his side in the night, his heart painful inside of him, the boy's face resting in his head.

∽

In the morning he felt oddly refreshed. The clothes he'd worn the day before chilled his skin as he dressed. Rain still hissed out the bedroom window, a slanting downpour, pounding the green grass grey.

He could see a woman crouched in a far corner of the backyard, facing away. She wore a hat with a brim like a lampshade, and in both hands she held some sharp, glinting instrument which she kept stabbing methodically at a black plot of soil, again and again, as if something were buried there that needed killing.

Sal watched for what felt like an intrusively long time, waiting for her to stop, he supposed, or turn around and notice him. After some minutes, he grew frightened at the idea that she would never notice him. With the points of his fingers he tapped on the glass, gently at first, then urgently, but the rain must have been too loud, or the woman too engaged in the violence of her task, for the sound to reach her. Sal wasn't even sure why he thought of her as a woman, since her long coat and wide hat concealed every part of her body. Finally, ashamed of how long he'd stood there watching, he turned away and tried to pretend to himself that he hadn't seen what he'd seen, that there was no one in the backyard.

The carpet in the living room soaked his feet. A flood had occurred overnight. Water slid in transparent streams down the wall beneath the window, dampening what boxes remained to be unpacked. But what alarmed Sal most of all was that there looked to be far too many boxes, each the same brown square tightly sealed by clear tape. He had no idea what they might contain, nor what the ones he'd spent yesterday unpacking had contained; the basement was just as bare as it had been when he arrived. What did he even own that might fit in a box?

He aimed to find out by taking one and opening it up when a knock came to the side door.

"It's me," a woman's voice called softly.

Sal went to the door and, opening it, discovered a dog sitting attentively on the far side. He had no idea about the various breeds of dogs, only that this one seemed a handsome, well-behaved animal, its wet dark hair sleek and shimmering, its hazel eyes regarding him impartially. When he bent to touch its head, it ducked through his legs and into the house.

Closing the door, Sal followed the dog to the bedroom, where it jumped up on the bed with its wet paws and settled itself comfortably on the pillow. Another knock came to the side door.

This time a woman stood where the dog had sat a moment ago. She wore a long dripping raincoat and held in her gloved hands a wide-brimmed hat. Strands of dark hair were plastered to her forehead and cheeks.

"I heard you were sick," she said, though at first Sal wasn't sure he'd heard her correctly. Her voice was terribly weak, and it was only after she'd spoken that he noticed how frail she appeared, her face so drawn it was almost the shape of the skull it concealed. He forgot how to speak.

"I said I heard you were sick," the woman repeated. She placed a hand on the doorframe for balance. "I'm here to see if you need anything."

"No," Sal said reassuringly. He felt prepared to catch the woman in the event that she collapsed. "At least I don't think so," he added, rather absurdly. "I might've been, but I'm fine now."

A spell of dizziness overcame him. He'd fled Farrow after what the newspapers had labeled a tragic accident and had gone somewhere else. But where? He remembered a TV in a soup kitchen, a reporter saying that the boy's name was Seamus. Pictures were shown of the parents, the funeral, the house. He'd stopped eating for a long time and had gotten sick, too sick to move or do anything but slip in and out of himself. How many days and nights had he spent in his truck this way? And yet here he was.

"When do you move in?" the woman asked. She kept her eyes on the hat she held, which she rotated continuously with nervous fingers.

"I got here yesterday," Sal said.

The woman nodded imperceptibly as she brushed by on her way inside.

Sal turned around. He'd been so captivated by the woman's appearance that he'd forgotten the flood, the dog, the boxes. Now he watched his guest drift about the living room, looking abstractedly at the bare walls and leaking window.

"We're just upstairs if you need anything," she said.

"That's very kind." Sal followed her to the bedroom. The dog looked up at them both as they entered, a torn corner of the pillowcase clamped between its teeth.

"You never mentioned a dog," the woman said, addressing her hat.

"It isn't mine," Sal insisted. "I don't think it's anyone's."

"I imagine it must be someone's."

Before Sal could explain, his eyes were drawn to the window beside the bed, out of which he could see the very same woman he'd been convinced stood next to him just now, crouched to her knees in the rain with her back to the house, savagely attacking the moist earth as though it had wronged her in some unspeakable way.

"I never approved of dogs myself," said the woman at his side, "though I suppose you're old enough now to do what you like."

But Sal failed to hear this, just as he failed to hear the reminder that he was to call upstairs should he need anything. It was only the sound of the side door banging shut that brought him back. He was alone. Nothing had changed, really—the dog still lay on the bed, eyeing him thoughtfully, white feathers from the torn pillow spread about the mattress—and yet he felt in his flesh that some awful shift had occurred, that the blood he could hear pumping in his ears did not belong to him, that the dog on the bed was not a dog, that there was a mind behind that protracted stare no animal could possess.

He looked away, but there seemed nowhere safe for his eyes to rest. The woman out the window brought him closer to panic the longer she did not leave.

On the floor at the foot of the bed sat a couple of empty boxes.

Picking one up, he tore off the top flaps, then the sides, and afterwards found some tape which he used to stick each piece to the window's glass, covering it completely. He listened carefully once he'd finished, his forehead pressed to the cardboard. The rain sounded louder as he held himself still in the damp dark, but the woman made no sound. For a second he was tempted to make sure she was still there before he stopped himself.

After a minute, he began to undress. It felt somehow wrong to turn a light on and attempt to make something of the day. The dog he'd momentarily forgotten hardly moved as he drew aside the covers and slid into bed. He wanted it gone but lacked the will to assert himself. All that was in his power was to lie down and wait for things to change—the day, his thoughts, himself, the maddening persistence of his own heartbeat.

~

The sound of footsteps reached him later that day, or perhaps it was another day. He had the sense they'd been there in his ears long before he'd really heard them, pattering about the ceiling to which his eyes were stuck.

When he tried to move his own feet, he couldn't feel them. He sat up to find the black weight of the dog heaped upon his shins. It neither stirred nor made a sound as he carefully extracted his legs. There was no sound he could hear but the footsteps overhead, continuous and hurried, at times almost frantic. The rain must finally have stopped.

Once freed, he pushed down the covers and shifted out of bed. Still the dog did not move, a motionless mound facing the near wall. Maybe it was dead, he thought without much interest. He put his clothes back on and left the room.

The power had apparently given out during his time in bed; the light-switch in the living room did nothing when he flicked it, and neither did the stove clock tell him the time. Out the window, the portion of sky he could see was a violet shade of grey, leading him to wonder whether the day was about to begin or had recently finished. He had a mind to go outside and test the air, but his shoes were nowhere to be found. For more than a minute he searched the suite, kicking aside sodden boxes and peering into cupboards. It came to him that he had no clear picture of what his shoes looked like, only that they must be somewhere, that he must have arrived wearing shoes of some kind.

It was a line of yellow light that ultimately distracted him. His search had brought him to the foot of the stairs beside his bedroom, a lighted slit glinting from the top door's bottom clearance. Placing a hand on the banister, he took the steps tentatively, not wanting to hear himself move.

"Hello?" he said to the door at the top.

"Come on in," a voice answered at once. He was too surprised to notice whether it sounded familiar.

Opening the door, he entered a kitchen. A man stood at the far end, bent over a sink, facing away, washing something in loud, steaming water. His hands, perhaps.

"Air's kept in if the door's kept closed," the man said without turn-ing, annoyed. "I know I've told you that before."

Sal closed the door behind him. It somehow wasn't obvious that the man at the sink was the same man who'd shown him the suite. He wore a worn brown housecoat ending at the knees, the back of his calves white as a trout's belly. Once he saw them, Sal could not take his eyes from the man's calves. If the lights were hit, he felt sure they'd glow.

"Done playing down there in the basement?"

Sal put a fist to his mouth and cleared his throat. "I only saw that your light was on," he said. "I came up to see about the power."

But the man wasn't listening, or else the water from the sink was too loud. Steam rose from the basin to encompass his lowered head.

A woman entered the room, appearing from a doorway to the man's left. She went to his side and kissed his shoulder. Sal reddened. He recognized her as the woman who'd paid him a visit earlier, only now her movements were defined by confidence and control. In place of a raincoat she wore a white blouse, the shoulders and back soaked by the wetness of her hair.

"Time to wash up," she said brightly. Sal watched as she crossed the room, took him by the wrist, and led him like a child to the sink. The man gave way, wiping his big red hands on his housecoat. It was indeed the man from before, Sal noticed, though he looked changed in some way. Sweat sheened the smooth dome of his head as he stepped aside.

"Sixty seconds," the woman instructed, forcing Sal's hands under the gushing faucet. They really were filthy. What had he done to dirty his hands in such a way? He watched with satisfaction the hot water turn brown as it spilled from his fingers and circled the drain. A bar of soap was given to him, which he rubbed between his palms until they were the colour they should be.

"Good enough," said the woman, taking away the soap and turning off the faucet. The silence was piercing. "How one pair of hands could ever get so grubby, I'll never know."

Sal dropped his eyes to his feet, embarrassed.

"Has anyone seen my shoes?" he asked suddenly.

"Don't tell me you've lost them," said the man. He had moved to the stove and was now stirring with a long wooden ladle the contents of a pot.

"I haven't lost them," Sal said, a vague panic building in his chest.

"Then show them to me."

"Just because I can't find them doesn't mean they're lost."

The man let out a deflated sigh.

"Let's leave it at that for now," the woman said. She took a chopping knife from a block on the counter and, with her back to Sal, began to hack at some unseen object placed on a cutting board before her, jabbing at it repeatedly. "Shamey, dear," she called over her shoulder, "would you be good enough to set the table?"

"What?" said Sal.

"You heard what," the man said. "Tables don't set themselves."

Sal's mouth hung open. For a moment there was no sound in the room but the knife on the cutting board and the ladle in the pot. The entire kitchen smelled of nothing.

"And where did your adventures take you today?" asked the woman.

"My adventures?"

"Please don't tell me you've been going back to that dead awful place. What's the name of it?"

"You mean Farrow?"

"God, what a hideous name for a place."

"It's no real place at all," said the man, stirring at the stove. "Hasn't been for years."

"Sounds so vulgar, more like a curse than a name."

"Places die out just like anything else."

"You better at least be wearing that helmet we gave you."

Sal kept quiet and still, imagining that he could evaporate into the air like the steam from the sink at his back.

"Did you check the basement?" the man asked.

"For what?" said Sal.

"For those shoes you lost."

Sal looked again at his feet. "I don't think so," he said, and began making his way obediently back toward the door.

"You'd better hurry," the woman said as he passed. "We're still waiting for that table to be set."

He paused for a moment, failing to articulate the questions swarming his head. Then he left the man and woman where they stood, closing the door behind him.

The basement suite had all but collapsed in his absence. Small sacks of moisture bulged and bubbled along the ceiling like the sores of diseased skin. When he looked to the window, he found most of it gone, a jagged hole you could almost crawl through giving way to the world outside. Bits of glass glinted in what was left of the carpet, which reeked of piss and mildew.

But the dog was just where he'd left it, alive and seemingly well, a partially eaten boot held in its forepaws. It sat up when he entered, and for a long moment Sal was held in place by a deeply questioning look.

"It's you that doesn't belong here," the dog surely meant to say.

Sal took the boot from its grip and found the other buried in the covers.

"I wish you'd tell me what you are," he said as he tied the laces. The dog only licked its face and readied itself for sleep. Sal left it alone.

The side door hung slanted from the top hinge and had to be kicked out. What struck him first as he stepped outside was the smell, a warm sea-stink he'd grown not only to tolerate but cherish, like the scent of his own soul. Leaving the ruins of the house behind, he walked a little ways down the road, past the husks of more structures that must once have housed lives, more of his memory slithering out in long strands with each step. It was enough now just to know this place where his life had led him and left him. Filling his lungs, he tasted salt.

ONE SYLLABLE, RHYMES WITH SIN

E.M. LINDEN

EDITORS' *Note: We regret this is the last in our* Traveller's Tales *series.*

The salt-lake is ten miles from K., although the distance changes with the desert's whims. (Dear Gwendoline, I know what you think. Stick to the facts! This is my final letter, so believe me. I have.)

Take a camel. Even in winter, horses die out here. The distances shimmer. Stay on the track, or you'll lose yourself to thirst and shifting sands.

(Something similar happened to me.)

The water's gone. But salt striates the sand, blazing white. And the desert stars are countless and brilliant as grains of sand and salt.

That's why people come. Some for adventure, some for the scenery, and some to earn their livings as porters, guides, chefs and navigators.

Others come for the stars. These, the star-hunters, set out from the caravanserai at dusk. They take flasks of smoky tea, and equipment swaddled like royals in infancy. They set up their contraptions, balance the legs of their telescopes on the sand, and unpack sextants and astrolabes from their camels' backs. When the desert turns cold (it is so cold at night, Gwen, I never felt cold until now), they hunt for stars. They hope to make a name for themselves out here. They hope to write their names into the skies, a kind of immortality.

And then, if they are really foolish, they send little missives about their expeditions back to London travel magazines.

Better to stay away.

Sometimes when the wind changes direction, or you scuff the sand with your boot, something gleams. Shattered glass from a telescope's eye. Bone fragments.

Those bone fragments belong to the lucky ones.

(I know that's not what our London readers wish to read.)

Stick to facts? My mouth is salt and sand. Sand scourges the cavern of my skull. Salt rimes my eye sockets and spine.

Stick to facts? I, too, sought immortality. Now I fear, most, that I will not die.

Stick to facts? *They* are here.

Don't name them. Say instead, *the ones of sand and salt.* Say: *the ones who sough like the wind over the dead lake.* Say: *one syllable, rhymes with sin.*

Or better still, say nothing. Spit in the fire, and stuff the cracks in your door with rags.

If you call them, they will come.

There is danger in names. Only the foolish and arrogant don't know it.

I was both.

I intruded on private rituals for my mocking dispatches. I sustained myself on the hospitality of strangers. I mined it twice, first to dine on; then to publish in your magazine. To amuse my readers and line my pockets. To impress you.

I laughed at local customs. I laughed at good advice. Advice that could, perhaps, have saved me.

I acted as though the stars were mine. As if I had discovered the desert.

I said *their* names.

I was very wrong, Gwen, about many things.

(I was not wrong about you.)

I thought science would tame the deserts. Even this one. Men of science and literature—in whose august company I unhesitatingly included myself—would render all its secrets safe and known. Astronomy, geography, and cartography would pin its shifting contours down, lifeless as a butterfly in a glass case.

I thought I was a man of science. I was too arrogant to recognize that the desert is where science was born—astronomy, geography, and cartography. Here, the skies outweigh centuries of human concerns, and navigation is the difference between water and death.

But even science has its limits.

The desert clarifies many things.

I scorned the people I travelled amongst, because they were superstitious. I have learned to my cost that *superstitious* does not mean *wrong*.

Gwen, I have made a living of trespass. And you rewarded me with your dry editor's praise. I craved the attention of your ink on my lines. That is no excuse.

Of all my trespasses, this, by the dead lake, did not seem the gravest.

I was wrong about that, too.

Erring is human. Forgiveness, also, is human. *They* do not forgive.

And they, too, can travel to other lands and take what they want. Like I did.

I am compelled to write to you one last time. (Yes, I say *compelled*. You are always reminding me to use words accurately.) Like a man before his execution, I write in full awareness of what comes next. I don't know if you will receive it—I must give it to the wind to take—but I think, somehow, you will. I think they want you to.

Because if you say their name, even if only in the silence of your own head, they will hear. One syllable, rhymes with sin. You are astute and love words and no doubt have already guessed.

And not just you. *Traveller's Tales* has decent circulation numbers, in London and beyond.

The facts, Gwen.

If you call them, they will come.

Perhaps they are already coming.

The stars are dark to me now. This is a farewell, and an apology.

Gwen, you have my heart. The rest of me walks the desert, ten miles from K.

THE HEALERS

ALEXANDER GLASS

WINTER HAD PUT him on the ground, and now winter had woken him. Had it not been for the snow, he might have seen the hole in the road, filled with dark water that was now turned to dark ice. The ice had seemed solid enough, and perhaps his horse could have navigated it, had it not shied, struck by fear. That was the last thing Peder remembered. The beast must have thrown him, and fled, taking with it his blanket roll, his shotgun and cartridges, his letter of introduction to the mayor in Moreau Rose, and—most importantly—his medical bag.

His water bottle, and a bundle filled with biscuit, were safe under his clothes. He had kept them there so that his body heat would keep them warm, along with a small bottle of brandy.

Propping himself up on one elbow, he peered along the track in both directions. His horse was nowhere to be seen, and the snow had filled its tracks. It might be waiting somewhere up ahead, but more likely had simply kept going, and he had no hope of catching up with it on foot.

Pain flared in his side as he hauled himself upright. There would be a glorious bruise along his ribs by morning.

He tugged out his pocket watch, his hands clumsy in their mittens —clumsy, too, from the cold, and from the still-tender scar on his right palm. It was past seven in the evening. His journey on foot would, he reckoned, take about four hours; but the road curved around to the west, and so he might shave off some time if he cut through the woods and met up with it later. So he climbed the earth-bank, which was not too high at this point, and set off between the dark spruces.

There was a trail leading approximately the right way, and so he followed it for a time, until to his surprise it opened up into a clearing. In the open space between the trees he came upon a wagon, a fire on the ground before it, a horse tethered to a nearby tree, and an old man sitting on a stump beside the fire, busying himself with a tin plate and a wooden spoon.

Peder smelled the wood-smoke, and something else, too, the heavy odour of some aromatic herb the old man must have thrown on to the fire; and behind that, something worse. Something the sweetness of the herb was supposed to hide. A harsh smell, something rotten; a dead animal, perhaps. Dead, or dying; the odour brought back memories of the infirmary back in the city, of patients with corrupted limbs or lungs, parts of them already decomposing even as they lived.

He raised a hand high as he came into the clearing, but the old man just grunted and nodded, having heard his snow-muffled tread already as he approached. The snow was still falling, but some of it was caught and held in the arms of the trees.

Drawing closer, Peder seated himself upon a mound, and stretched out his hands to the fire. The night stepped back behind the circle of trees.

"Lost your way?"

Peder shook his head. "Lost my horse, and everything it was carrying. Even my doctor's bag. If I'm lucky the animal's bolted all the way to Moreau Rose, and I might catch up with it there."

"You've come at the wrong time for food," the old man observed. "All that's left in the pot are the scraps and the fat."

"I'll trade the scraps and fat for some good biscuit," Peder said, and broke his packet in two, handing over the larger portion of it in exchange for the plate and spoon. He dropped his biscuit into the pot and let it soak in the juice for a few moments before emptying the pot on to the plate. The old man sniffed at the bundle he had received with evident satisfaction, then tucked it away.

"You're a physician, then?"

"I am. I was told Moreau Rose was in need of one."

The old man laughed, and then coughed, a sound much like that of the wood snapping in the fire. "Not right now, mister. Not any longer. They just got healed."

Peder paused, the spoon part-way to his mouth. "By whom?"

"By me." The old man grinned, but there was a sourness in it. He glanced back at the wagon, and Peder followed his gaze. Painted on its side in curlicued green, as if for a carnival attraction, were two words: *The Healers*.

A snake-oil man, Peder guessed. He had heard that the Chinese had an oil that actually had some effect, extracted from a water-snake—not a miracle cure, but something that soothed the body and stimulated the mind. Rattlesnake or viper oil had no such effect, and anyway most of these hucksters were selling simple opium elixir if the suckers were lucky, or more likely just coloured syrup.

The old man coughed again, his body shaking with it, then took in a shuddering breath, and wiped his mouth on his sleeve. Peder guessed that, in fact, the town would still be in need of a doctor after all. Without his bag, he had no real remedies to offer, so instead he brought out the brandy bottle and handed it across.

The smell was still swirling about the clearing. Now that he was closer to the old man, Peder decided it was not coming from him. He was unwashed, that was all. The horse, then? He examined it from where he sat; it was underfed, probably ill-used, but seemed as healthy as could be expected for its situation. Something else, then. He peered again at the wagon, wondering whether the old man had a companion, a shill, as such men often did. A keen irony, he thought, if the sellers of quack medicines could not heal themselves.

A sound came from inside the wagon, a thump, followed by a wordless cry. The old man turned and growled something, a harsh rebuke—Peder didn't catch the words, even assuming they were in a language he knew—and was met with silence.

"Well." The old man produced a clay pipe, knocked out the dottle, and began to pack it from a pouch. "I'm stopping for the night. Just here to get off the road."

And not to be found by any irate townsfolk, Peder added silently to himself, once they realize the potation they doubtless paid a pretty penny for has no real effect at all. A doubt nagged at him, though, unwelcome and unexpected. If the shill was bedridden, unable to play the part of a man wondrously healed, and the old man himself was sickening, why would anyone have believed their patter?

"I'll be on my way then," he said, though the ache in his side was beginning to tell, and he did not relish the journey ahead. He should have risen at once, and taken his leave; but curiosity got the better of him. Curiosity, and a touch of resentment against these people who profited from pain. In his mind, there was nothing worse than a snake-oil man. "Good business, was there?"

The old man looked up sharply; then his gaze softened, and his lip curled. He thought he had found a kindred spirit. "Good enough. Same as it is in all these towns. Accidents. Injuries. Lost fingers, lost eyes. Burns. Toothache. Fevers, of course. And the pox, always the damned pox.

"I said 'towns'—but truthfully they're still not much more than the mining camps they started out as, up here; or the farmsteads and trading posts they were, down on the edge of the plain.

"The boy, there," he said, tipping his head at the wagon, "he always wanted to learn medicine, since he was knee-high. Wanted to help people, make the fevers go away. Ever since a fever came and carried off his mother." He grunted, chewed on something, once. "No need, in the end. No need for learning. No need for doctoring. We do what we do, and then we move on.

"We've made enough to live like kings," he went on, and Peder frowned at the bitterness in his voice—it didn't fit with his words, until he added, "And yet we can't, not really. Where am I supposed to take him? What can I do with him? All that money, and I can't spend it. All we can do is keep moving. When he dies—if he ever dies—I suppose I'll get to enjoy my reward. Not before that."

The old man blinked, frowning, realizing that he had been talking to himself at the end, maybe saying things he wouldn't want a stranger to hear.

"Must be the liquor talking," he said, weakly, and handed back the bottle.

Again, Peder knew he should walk away, but again anger kept him there. "So you take people's money, and then you flee in the night before they know they've been cheated."

The old man held his gaze for a moment, a sneer fixed on his mouth. Then he looked away, and spat into the fire.

"You're well-dressed for the wild, friend. Where did the money for that come from? Are you telling me you won't be charging a good fee for your work?"

"I intend to make a living. But I do it to help others. It sounds like your son wanted to do the same, before you taught him better."

"I taught him—*tried* to teach him—that helping others won't do you any good. It just means you take on their pain."

"So you rob them instead. I guess *that* does you some good."

"You think they've been robbed? All right, boy. All right. I'll tell you who's been robbed.

"My Clara died one summer, and after she was stolen from me I couldn't stand to live in that town any more. So we left, the boy and me. Travelled through the winter. We passed alongside a frozen river— you know the way the water mutters and growls to itself underneath the ice? It sounds like it's warning you away. Maybe it was. If so I didn't hear, or didn't understand.

"I sent the boy down to break some of the ice and bring it back in the cooking pot. I stayed with the cart and made a fire. I had matches, but finding dry wood in winter was the Devil's own work. I had some birch-bark, good for kindling, better than paper, even, but that was all. I found some dry grass in the shadow of the trees and some sticks and twigs that the water had carried up the bank, back in the fall. And then I sat there feeding a young flame, with the wind laughing at me.

"Just as I had it going, the boy came back, and surprised me. I didn't hear him—too busy with what I was doing. But I looked up, and there he was, out of nowhere, with the shards of ice poking out of the cooking pot, and with the fire reflected in his eyes. I shouted out a curse, and I jumped back; and my hand went into the fire.

"It burned so quickly. Grease in the cloth, I guess. My sleeve, my whole arm up to the elbow, was like a brand. I fell into the snow, and I rolled on top of my arm, and with my other hand I packed more snow on to it. I felt so sick, even as I was doing it. I won't tell you what the skin looked like, what it smelled like.

"The boy came close, and looked me in the eye, and somehow I knew that he understood what to do about it. He put his hand on the burns—and they were gone.

"Well. Not gone.

"Someone was screaming. For a second I thought it was me. Then I realized it was the boy. His arm was all burned. It was the same injury. Exactly the same. He'd healed my arm, but the only way he could do it was to take the burn on to himself.

"You don't have to believe it. I don't care if you do. But I'm no snake-oil man. His cure works. And I don't hide it—what he is, or what will happen when one of those fine people touches him, what will happen to their wound or their fever or their pox, where it will go. How he will suffer. They know. They all know. And they pray for him, and they curse me for taking their coin. But they pay, and they lay hands on him to be healed."

There was a long silence, broken only by the chuckle of the fire and the sound of the falling snow, like small, soft kisses.

At last Peder said, "Let me see him."

"You don't want to do that. You can't heal him. No one can."

Rising to his feet, Peder pulled the heavy woollen mitten from his right hand, and held it up with the fingers stretched out. Across the palm, written in livid red flesh, was a scar. The skin, even now, was tender and thin.

"There was a woman in the infirmary," he said, and his voice was quiet, empty of feeling. "She… No, never mind the story of it."

The story still troubled him. An accident, she insisted, but it looked like a defensive wound, and he had wondered whether he was treating her and sending her back to the person who had cut her; and there was nothing he could do to heal that.

"I took her hand, only to examine the wound, that's all. And then I was dizzy for a moment, and when I recovered myself, the wound was gone. Gone from her, I mean. And there I was, holding the wound in my hand."

He held up the hand a moment longer, and then lowered it, and drew the mitten back over the scar.

The old man looked away, drawing his coat closer about himself, as Peder went over to the wagon. The smell was stronger, here, and he approached with one arm over his mouth and nose. There were two steps up to the door. He climbed up, and pulled it open, and a small sound escaped his lips.

Inside the wagon, he saw only two things.

To one side, he saw a chest. He did not know what it contained, but he could hazard a guess.

To the other, he saw a shape—or rather, something that had once had a shape.

The smell was overpowering, now, bringing saliva to the back of his mouth and a roiling nausea to his gut.

He wondered how many towns the old man had visited, how many coins had changed hands and gone into the chest, how many wounds and infections had been passed from his customers to the boy. To the old man's son. And the boy bore the marks of them all.

"All right," came the old man's voice from behind him. "You've seen him now. No charge for that, between friends. Now come away."

He coughed again, and Peder realized that even he—something worse than a snake-oil man, a walking corruption on the body of the world—had been unable to bring himself to pass his own sickness on to his son. That much humanity remained in the old man, if all else was gone.

The snow was falling more heavily now. It would lie deep by morning. A mote of it flew into Peder's eye, and he blinked; but it seemed to him that he saw more clearly, then. Once again, winter had woken him.

Trembling, perhaps from the cold, he drew the mitten from his hand. He did not know what would happen if he touched the thing in the wagon. He could imagine various outcomes, none of them good. But he knew now that he could not leave the boy without trying to help him. He reached out, into the darkness of the wagon—as he imagined countless customers had done before him—until he felt skin, warm and clammy, beneath his palm. At once his head grew light, and then the shadows in the wagon reached out and claimed him.

When he came to he was lying in the dark. It took him a moment to understand, after he opened his eyes, that he was on the floor of the wagon. His pocket watch had rolled away from him, hurled from its pocket as his clothes had split, as his changing body had torn its way out of the fabric. He felt the pain in his side, still, but now it was only one voice in a chorus of hurt.

The shape he had seen—the boy—was gone. He was alone in the wagon.

The corrupt smell was still about him; but now it was emanating from his own swollen, rotting form.

Somewhere behind him he could hear raised voices, one younger, one older. The younger was enraged, the older protesting at first, pleading, wheedling, then screaming, and screaming again. A dull clang might have been the pot falling from its stand, the last of the scraps and the fat spilling into the fire.

He closed his eyes, as the herb-sweet smoke from the campfire became entwined with the smell of the old man's burning flesh.

After a time he heard footsteps approaching, and a cough: the boy had taken that from his father, a last act of healing before his revenge.

He wondered what the boy would decide to do with him.

DEAD MAIDEN CHIC

BARBARA A. BARNETT

IT'S cute how people think I'm dead. Leapt from a parapet. Drank poison. Drowned in a river. Went mad from guilt or grief or both. There are so many versions—which should be your first clue that no one's gotten the story quite right. Yet still you search for me in their poems and their songs, hoping to trap me anew in one of your own.

Which laughable reason for my supposed death do you prefer? She was too fragile for this world? Too delicate? Pretty words that sound better than what they mean: "She's dead because she was a chick, and chicks can't hack it, am I right?"

I'll grant you the poetics. In a way, I did die casting that body off. It never fit right. Lacked pockets. And all that maintenance—sleeping and eating and bathing, yet even that wasn't enough. I still had to brush colored powders on top of that papery white skin to look acceptable. Pretty.

That's why no one recognizes me now. They couldn't conceive of a life for me beyond that body. Except you. That's why I've become that cold breath on your neck on an otherwise warm day. That moan from the floorboards when you're alone in the house. That phantom whisper imploring you to write me a different ending.

Sometimes you think you've caught a glimpse of me, and sometimes you're right. But it was like that before the funereal flowers and the odes to my beauty. People were so damn certain they saw me, but only on rare occasion truly did. And when they see what I've become ... well, let's just say that some people *do* leap to their deaths out of madness.

But I didn't. It wasn't madness, nor was it heartbreak over a man who died or killed my brother or married another woman. Leave a body behind and people make all sorts of assumptions, don't they?

No, I'd merely outgrown my clothing. And why keep wearing something uncomfortable when you can take it off? Well, there *are* reasons—how else to explain high heels—but in my case, the pretty outfit was no longer worth being treated like a little girl.

Girl. I'm fond of that term even though it's not accurate anymore. Like those stories about my death, it paints a pretty, tragic picture, inviting people to look closer in their search for another Ophelia-esque victim to venerate. It never occurs to them that *they* could be the victim.

Oh, don't worry, not you. I wouldn't want to ruin that outfit. It has pockets. Besides, I've tried bodies like yours, and little ever changes. I'm simply given new roles to suit each costume. Roles like the one you chafe at. The one that tells you compassion is weakness.

I'll be honest: at first I came here because I thought your body would be a better fit than the last one. But then I caught a glimpse of the person I used to be, neither victim nor monster, emerging in your words. Words you just erased. Words you fear will mark you as less than a man.

Perhaps what we need to truly break free is each other—you to write me a new story, me to give you the courage. The clichés have their uses, yes, but dead maiden chic feels so yesterday, don't you think?

SUBSIDENCE

STEVE RASNIC TEM

EVENTUALLY HE REALIZED his only power was letting go. Kurt bought the small house a year into Jane's illness. Not long ago she'd been fine, but nature was unpredictable, and sometimes a vicious saboteur. They needed a single-story home because she couldn't manage stairs. They had to get rid of three-fourths of their possessions to fit into the new place. Jane was past caring, and he made himself not care as he sold, gave away, or donated things he had loved for decades. But he kept her dolls and animal ceramics, artificial flower arrangements and woven wall hangings. He couldn't imagine living in a house without them.

He kept asking what she wanted. But she said she wasn't making any more decisions. It frightened him to hear that. For a while there'd been a wandering problem. The space in a smaller home would be easier to control. On good days she looked fine, but terrible things were happening beneath the surface.

At least it was a lovely house. It had a glow about it. Its roots went deep. People had lived here for a century. They were next in a long line of lives spent in this singular location. He tried to find out about former occupants, but no records were available.

Kurt held onto enough antiques to furnish their new home. They fit right in with the mission-style built-ins and trim. Out of their once vast library he saved two hundred volumes. At the end of the street was a fine old branch library. He hoped they could walk down there together. She no longer read but enjoyed it when he read to her.

But Kurt had always been too optimistic about her illness. Following the strain of the move Jane deteriorated rapidly, sinking both physically and mentally. Most days he was lucky to get a simple *Hello* out of her. The visiting nurse said she was stable, but honestly, she wasn't likely to live the year. Kurt spent hours at her bedside, searching for vague recollections of who she used to be. He knew there was nothing to be done, and the coldness of the knowledge infuriated him.

He didn't go out. He never left the house. He had all their groceries delivered, including fresh cut flowers he put in a vase on her dresser. He didn't know if she ever noticed them.

Six months into their residency Kurt first noticed the cracks. He thought they were cobwebs at first. He couldn't afford a housekeeper, and even with a long-handled duster he found it difficult to reach distant crevices. But climbing a ladder—something his doctor had forbidden him to do—he could see them clearly: dozens of tiny cracks in the corners where walls and ceilings met, around lintels, around heating vents. Defects, fractures, worrying signs.

There were other issues, phenomena he couldn't explain. Rising and falling water in the toilets, faucets coming on for no reason, doors swinging open, curtains fluttering even when the windows were shut. Jane hadn't noticed as far as he knew, and he wasn't about to tell her.

He'd been initially concerned because this house sat lower than the others in the neighborhood, although the drop did make it feel nicely secluded. His yard was at least a foot lower than the public sidewalk, necessitating a few concrete steps down to his front walk.

Kurt hadn't yet investigated the basement. The stairs were dimly lit and appeared to descend forever. He stood at the top and attempted to smell for dampness. He smelled something else, but he didn't think it was damp.

A little settling was to be expected. He didn't have time for this. Kurt's focus had been, and continued to be, his wife, watching her responses or lack thereof, reading to her, playing music, even singing to her in his off-key, cracked voice. Sometimes she spoke, and sometimes her words made sense, but not always. He imagined she was already far along on her own personal journey, her mind in two different worlds.

When Kurt needed a break, he went out on the front porch and sat watching the people passing by. A lot of students headed to and from the library. A few older couples strolling by holding hands. They sometimes smiled and waved. Each time he was inordinately touched.

He lowered his eyes to his front walk and thought it looked off. The edges weren't straight. It had what? Folded? He got out of his chair and walked toward the street. There was a definite slant. A crack a good half-inch wide crossed the width of the concrete. The halves of the walk dipped as if it were a ship broken in two and sinking.

"It looks like subsidence." His name was Tom, a friend of a friend, someone who worked in construction, and a man who'd offered to examine Kurt's house for free, because Kurt's wife was dying.

"What's that?" Kurt asked. He was embarrassed. He was well-read, but he didn't know the word.

"The ground sinks because materials are moving underneath where you can't see them. It can take a while to notice something is wrong. Day to day, everything looks normal, but there's shifting, gaps developing, breakage, in the dark places unknown to you. Then one day your world collapses."

He roamed the house with Kurt in tow, examining diagonal cracks in the walls, ceilings, and brickwork. In the spare bedroom which Kurt used when Jane's tossing didn't allow him to sleep, Tom found rippling in the wallpaper. He checked all the doors and windows and pointed out where the sticking—which Kurt had noticed but ignored— might be indicative of a bigger problem.

"Your door and window frames are out of true. This house has shifted significantly."

They descended into the basement. Kurt was still hesitant, but Tom persuaded him he needed to see any problems with his own eyes. Even with the light on they required a flashlight. The steps took them all the way to the far wall of the basement. Kurt counted twenty-five.

"I've never seen such a deep basement under a house this age," Tom said. "At least you have a solid staircase." He pointed his flashlight at the stairs. "That's not going anywhere." The treads were thick, solid wood, supported by a substantial mass of concrete.

"I'm not seeing any cracks or separations down here, no signs of damp, no salt deposits on the walls." He jumped up and down. "But there shouldn't be this much give in the floor. It's as if it's unattached, floating. I don't get it."

They investigated every corner, swinging the flashlight at bare walls, the floor, the spider-like furnace hiding in the shadows. The basement was empty and surprisingly dust and cobweb free. Tom started back up the stairs. Kurt had to scramble to keep up.

Back in the kitchen Tom gave him a card. "This guy is a good soils test engineer." He gave him another. "This woman is a foundation expert. They'll tell you what you need to do."

Kurt stuck the cards in his wallet and thanked him, even though he had no intention of calling anyone. Experts charged money he didn't have and prescribed solutions he wouldn't be able to afford. What were the odds of the house falling down before both he and Jane died?

~

The hardest part of taking care of her was knowing he was powerless to change anything. What was going to happen was going to happen. Human beings were too fragile and died too easily. They suffered from a failure of design.

The house made more sounds at night than their former home. Perhaps because it was older. Everyone knew old houses made noise. But Kurt now knew it was also not geometrically sound. This house moaned and groaned, its movements impersonating knocks, rapping, and footsteps. His eyes weren't what they used to be, but the walls appeared to move at night. They breathed. At times they shuddered.

Kurt never knew at the start of any day how aware Jane would be, or how willing to communicate. This had negligible effect on the activities he did for her: changing her clothes, combing her hair, clipping her nails, brushing her teeth, cleaning up her accidents.

Swallowing water tended to sicken her, but her lips were cracked, her mouth almost empty of saliva. He gave her chipped ice, experimenting until he found a size which wouldn't make her choke.

He gave her small bits of food he knew she could manage, delivering them slowly as if they were a sacrament. Every time she coughed, he was afraid she was choking.

He gave her pills four times a day, tracked and checked off a list. There were other pills for pain to be delivered as needed. These frightened him because he didn't want to give her too much—he might kill her—and yet he couldn't sit there while she was in agony.

One night she cried in his arms, incoherent, delirious, but he had given her the maximum. Was now the time to give her more? The moment passed, but Kurt knew it would come around again, her distorted mouth, her slurred calls for relief. There was no escaping it. If she asked him to help her die, what would he say?

Some days she slept for hours and woke up frightened and confused, not knowing where she was or the day. One night she sat up and stared at him. "I don't think we'll ever make love again." She began to cry. He held her in his arms and stroked her head.

Most nights he stayed in bed with her no matter how restless her sleep. He knew he couldn't go on like this. He would have to move into the other room. Already he had trouble staying awake during the day.

The nurse explained in grim detail what he should expect as Jane's death approached. She described how her breathing would change as mucous and saliva built up in her throat, how awful it would sound, as if she were in terrible pain, but he needed to understand she was not. This would likely last for only a few hours before her heart and lungs stopped.

He didn't believe he could listen or sit there watching. He couldn't lie in bed with her while that terrible transformation occurred. He was ashamed of himself. All she'd ever asked of him was to be with her at the end.

He lay down in the bed and pulled her against him. She woke him sometime later, coughing, pleading for water. He went to the sink and ran the cold faucet. But a fine sediment covered the bottom of the glass.

~

Not long after, Jane fell headlong into delirium.

She kept insisting she heard sounds coming from the basement and would Kurt please check it out. He could have told her he checked and found nothing wrong. She had no way of verifying. He didn't want to tell her he was afraid to go down there.

She claimed there were people in the room when he left her alone, so if he didn't want any uninvited visitors in their home he should always be where she could see him. She was more alert than he'd seen her in weeks, but it seemed cruel her alertness was tied to her delusions. She babbled on about what these invisible presences were doing, and ordered him to listen, because they were sending them a warning.

Kurt didn't know if the illness was causing her delirium, or if it was the result of being in bed for weeks on end with the same lighting and the same environment. The sameness can do terrible things to a mind. Sometimes he'd open the window, and she would turn her head in that direction, like a plant turning toward the light.

He asked her simple questions to ground her, random facts about their life together, names of parents and schools. She forgot more than she remembered, and what she did remember was often colored in deep paranoia. *These creatures*, as she called them, meant them serious harm. "Don't you understand? They're so far above us, to them we're a small, forgettable meal."

Her stomach became swollen. Kurt didn't like to think about what might be inside. She was burning up. Sweat saturated the sheets.

She was charged with an ineffable emotional electricity. Just being around her infected him. If he sat with Jane too long, he began to see a complication of shadows parading across the walls, but he couldn't match up those shadows with anything physically present.

At one point she reached over and grabbed the glass off the bedside table, shattered it on the edge, and held a shard to her throat. Kurt snatched it out of her hand, giving himself a deep cut. He wrapped his hand in a towel from the bed. She'd collapsed back into her pillow, comatose. He saw no signs of breathing. Her dolls watched him from across the room urging him to do something. But he didn't know what to do. In desperation he slapped Jane across the face, the first time he'd even thought of hitting his wife. She opened her mouth and made this shrill, inhuman sound. He crawled on top of the blood-stained sheets and held her, chanting "I'm sorry I'm sorry I'm sorry." The dolls across the room chanted with him.

The day was extraordinarily long. He picked up the phone to call 911, but got no dial tone, instead hearing waves of electrical static. There was no longer a clock in the bedroom—Jane said it whispered unpleasant things—so he had no idea how long they'd lain there. A myriad of sounds slipped into the room, but he did not look around to see what they were. Eventually she fell asleep, and he climbed off the bed and went into the bathroom to clean himself up. Thankfully, the cut wasn't as deep as he'd thought. He poured peroxide over it and tied a crude bandage on. He pulled some fresh sheets from the laundry cabinet but didn't know how to change the bed without waking her, and the last thing Kurt wanted to do was awaken Jane.

When he walked back into the bedroom he saw those spirits, those creatures, leaping from the bed and into the fractured walls of the room. He did not believe in ghosts. He never had. And it strangely reassured him these were not ghosts. These forms—rippling, multiple-appendaged, with too many orifices to count—had obviously never been human at all.

The room itself had changed. What had been solid had become soft and ill-defined. Much of what had been invisible, the very air, appeared intermittently opaque and crystallized.

Kurt experienced severe vertigo. He sat down on the floor. From this angle the ceiling appeared to have retreated. There was a fluttering and a grinding of translucency along its edges. He became aware of a terrible stench, both salty and sulphurous. He'd never smelled anything like it. The floor began to slant.

From her high perch on the bed, Jane leered down at him. "This isn't even *our* home; did you know that? The realtor had no right to sell it to us. This is *their* home. They've lived underneath this house forever."

Her shadow, cast on the wall behind the bed, began to change.

Kurt didn't recall falling asleep, but when he woke up, he was lying on the floor in front of the bed, using the clean folded sheets as a pillow. There was light in the room. He assumed he must have slept through until the next day.

He got to his feet and checked on Jane. She was deep in sleep, her breathing relaxed. She was covered in dried blood, his, he presumed. He got a wet sponge from the bathroom and tried to clean her. She began to sputter and choke so he stopped. She opened her eyes and gazed at him.

"They've become so bold," she said. "So obnoxious."

"Who?"

"Why the souls, silly." She smiled at him as if he were a child. "They slip out of the cracks in our house, showing themselves even while I'm looking right at them. As if my opinion doesn't matter. Don't you think that's a bit cheeky?"

Of course, he'd seen them as well. Maybe her dying body had contaminated him. He wondered how long these presences had been here. There were so many limits on what humans could know. Most of his so-called knowledge was simply an interpretation of the facts.

Kurt felt a shift in gravity, a difference in the air. Everything had changed somehow, yet he knew his wife was still dying. Everything else about this strange day was extraneous.

She heaved an enormous sigh which reverberated throughout the room. The walls shook with it. He was terrified. He wasn't ready yet.

A painful light issued from the cracks in the walls, revealing new openings he hadn't noticed before. He looked at the window. It was still dark outside. What he had mistaken for a new day was the light leaking from somewhere below.

The wallpaper began to sag as more brilliance shone through. The light manifested as a fabric unravelling into strings as it traveled through the air. Its salient aspects were its intensity, and the insignificance it made him feel.

The light crossed his arm, searing the skin. The pain made him howl, even though he tried to contain it. Jane's eyes moved as if she were searching for him. But he was standing right in front of her. He watched as the radiating fabric dropped onto the furniture, over the vase full of flowers, her small collections of ceramic animals and dolls. Everything the fabric touched developed its own glow, as if they were on fire. If their house were to burn down now, he couldn't think of anything he'd care to salvage.

The light scraped her skin. There was a scent of copper. She began to bleed. The pillow wrapped around her neck like a bloated scarf. Had they decided to kill her?

The folds of light twisted into non-humanoid suggestions, shapeless, or at least in forms difficult to comprehend, segmented bags of translucent alien viscera, gigantic cilia, liquid flowing carapace. These things traveled across the room, appearing to sample every location in curiosity or some mysterious quest for satiation. Periodically they emitted dazzling waves of light which scoured the walls. Where the light hit the floor it turned to steam, leaving behind an ashen stain.

The house shook itself as if sentient, struggling for protection, attempting to sever itself from whatever occupied it. The flowers on her dresser expanded, sending out long, ornate stalks and curling tendrils, the blossoms opening and closing like mouths. The dolls began to gossip amongst themselves, grabbing the whimpering ceramic animals and chewing them to bits.

Jane began that terrible choking rasp, the tortured rattle the nurse warned him about. Her body shook under the power of it. Kurt had feared this moment, and now he was terrified of her. He'd promised her he would stay and was mortified he could not. He turned to leave, and she jumped out of bed and snarled at him. He ran.

She scrambled after him, her face wrapped in a glowing sheen. They scuffled. He felt a sharp pain. She was biting into his side.

He extricated himself from her hands. It felt like she had more than two. He ran through the doorway and slammed the door shut behind him, pressing his shoulder against it to keep it closed. She began beating on it.

The door felt silky just before it came apart. He ran down the hall. She was close behind him, running on all fours. The silkiness spread to the walls around him, then a silvery damp spilling across the floor. Then they were out into the shambles of the living room, where the furniture had become piles of glistening sludge.

The lines between walls and ceiling began to smear. Kurt glanced back. Her face had become smooth and featureless.

The house was twisting, angles altering, tiles popping off the kitchen floor, every plane transforming as if to reveal the secret architecture underneath. Distortion popped the basement door open. Kurt went through it, not considering the basement's dead end.

He was almost to the bottom of the basement staircase, and he couldn't hear her anymore. He grabbed the railing and twisted around. He could see her head at the top of the stairs, watching him. He wondered if she was going to follow, or seal him inside the basement.

~

Kurt descended the staircase, but instead of finding the floor, he was at the top of yet another staircase. He couldn't go back up the stairs because of Jane, or whoever it was who waited, so he continued. A force, a kind of suction, drew him down the stairs.

He found himself on another landing, a deeper darkness beyond that landing, and more steps leading down. The light above, shining from the basement door, appeared to be shrinking. He himself was shrinking it seemed. He was a tiny presence on these enormous stairs.

Outside the walls of the basement, he could feel the ground and everything in it moving, taking the house somewhere new. He continued walking down. He tried to control his breathing, hoping to take in no more than a small sample of air at a time. He had his doubts about the safety of the atmosphere.

There was some variation in the basement walls the further he descended, differentiations in strata and composition. Any variety of stability seemed forever out of reach.

Several more flights of stairs and he could no longer see any light above. He had no idea how he could see at all. He concluded the basement walls contained some inherent illumination, too subtle for him to perceive its source.

The staircase lost its proper scale, either too large for the space or too small. Now and again, he thought the stairs were tilting. He seized the railing and held on tight. But he was old and not strong. The staircase began to spiral.

There was a sudden, explosive shock as the stairs ended. He was standing on the basement floor. The concrete was sandy beneath his feet, as if it were beginning to disintegrate. The floor began to smolder.

He looked down. He saw them there through the not so solid floor, their incomprehensible silhouettes, swimming or flying through that unfamiliar medium. There was nothing sane about it. His final hours had become a time of great discovery and a loss of innocence.

The police were called for a welfare check when a large grocery delivery remained on the porch for weeks without being taken inside. Squirrels had ravaged the contents, and the officer who responded to the call had to chase off a family of racoons before he could get to the door. He knocked and pounded for some time. He then announced his presence and broke in.

It was a small, well-furnished home. Somewhat secluded because the ground was lower than the street. Mission style or Craftsman. He didn't know the difference, but it felt comfortable and welcoming. The beds in both bedrooms were unmade, but the rooms were otherwise clean and orderly. The second bedroom included a bookcase full of antique books with strange titles. The light coming through the windows was warm and pleasant. It made the polished wooden floors glow. The main bedroom displayed several collections: dolls and ceramics, dusted and well-cared-for. There was a vase on the dresser for flowers. He assumed a woman lived here.

There was no food in the house, and no sign of the occupants. A door in the kitchen led to the basement. He stood at the top of the stairs and looked down into the darkness. He pulled out his flashlight, then reconsidered. The steps appeared to go on forever. He decided that taking those steps wasn't his job.

AN ANTIQUE PUZZLE CHEST OF UNKNOWN PROVENANCE

NEIL WILLIAMSON

"IT'S a handsome piece of furniture, I'll give you that," Isabel says, smoothly covering the fact that she'd just been about to sit her wine glass down on the chest's golden lacquer, and only at the last second thought the better of it. She settles for running her fingers casually over the wood instead, briefly tracing the intricate geometric inlays. Pretending only passing interest. I can tell she's intrigued, though, if wary. Which is fair. I would be.

"Must have come as a surprise!" she goes on. "When Marcie and *I* were married, she barely mentioned Uncle Henry's name. We certainly never visited. Wouldn't have thought she'd have featured in the will at all, let alone end up with something like *this*."

The chest is an impressive beast. It squats, powerful and poised, like a sumo wrestler, the blonde wood glowing. The silken grain renders the ancient mortice and tenons all but invisible, although they're by far the most mundane of the secrets of its construction. The exquisite maze of marquetry applied to every surface conceals count-less drawers and doors, and things that look like drawers and doors, but aren't; and things that are, but don't look like much of anything at all. A little patient probing will reveal that there are hidden buttons and flush-set levers. There are secret springs and magnets. Things that slide and swivel, and things that pop soundlessly open under just the right pressure.

You spend enough time with it and the chest will reveal itself to you. It invites your attention. Seductive, to the right sort of people. Me? I've never been that kind of people. But even I've become appreciative of the thing. Curious, even. Morbidly so.

No one in the family knows the chest's origin. The appraiser Marcie got in was adamant that it was neither Italian nor Japanese, nor was it Malaysian or Edwardian English. He tried to convince us that meant it had to be a modern piece and offered pennies for it, but his eager, restless eyes gave away the greedy lie.

Not that I could sell it now anyway. For any price.

The chest lives in our little living room, bang in front of the TV. That was Marcie's doing, of course, once the obsession kicked in, but I don't think I'll bother moving it. I prefer to stream shows in bed and, for better or worse, there's no one to complain about my midnight horror binges now.

"Yeah," I say. "It *was* a surprise. Although…" I laugh. Does it sound as fake as it feels? "I'm not sure it was really intended as *a reward*."

I only met Uncle Henry once at the funeral of another of Marcie's barely-acknowledged relatives. Things were already on the slide between me and Marcie even then and the shrewd old man had seen it right away, though it would be months before I'd catch up with the script. I only realized later, looking back, that the chief seasoning to our brief and quite pleasant conversation at the egg sandwich end of the buffet had been pity.

Instead of meeting my gaze, Isabel intensifies her focus on one of the knobs she's been examining.

"How do you mean?" she says, taking another sip of wine, leaving a lipstick smear on the rim. It's an uncommon shade, but nevertheless recently familiar to me. You wouldn't think two super smart people would fall for the oldest cliché in the book, would you?

"Oh," I say, amazed at the brightness in my tone, "Old Henry probably just wanted to frustrate Marcie with a challenge she couldn't solve. I did say on the phone that it was a puzzle chest, didn't I?" Picking up the bottle of Malbec, I enjoy its tempting heft for a moment. "Top up?" When Isabel nods I splash red into her glass. "You know what she's like," I finish with a smile.

"Oh, yeah, I remember," she's careful to say, arching her brows in mock solidarity for good measure. "Cheers!"

She must have twigged by now, but she's still sticking with the pretence. *Jesus*, but this is hard.

I sip my wine. Watching her. Her feather cut bob is growing out and doesn't look like it's had much more than a quick brush today. The lovely English-mustard-coloured cardigan, neat around her skinny shoulders, hasn't been depilled in a while. And her earlobes sport plain fake-pearl studs that would look old on someone her mother's age, let alone her own. None of it goes; it's taking-the-bins-out presentable and no more. Of course, it's only me she's meeting after all. Dull, dowdy Nora. Why even bother? It's not like I'm competition.

She isn't even aware of my scrutiny. Her attention is back on the chest, the allure magnified the moment I dropped the P-word again. Because, like Marcie, she's a puzzler. Obsessed by crosswords, sudokus, acrostics, logic problems. *Nora has one more spouse than Isabel. Marcie will really pretty soon have no spouse at all.* Their perfect night in during their two years together was cosying up with *Midsomer Murders* while laying down the big scores in *Words With Friends*. Playing games, second guessing. It's no foundation for a marriage, is it? Theirs was never going to last, and it didn't.

None of that for me, thanks. Nothing concealed here and no ulterior motives. I thought Marcie appreciated that. She always said she did. *Isabel was so Machiavellian, Nora,* she told me once. I'd had to look it up.

I just can't be bothered with mysteries. The lying and cheating. The drama. At least, that *was* the case… But needs must.

Honestly? I'd really love nothing more than to be able to admire this beautiful old chest simply because it looks nice. Because of the amazing craftsmanship that went into making it. Even, yes, because those little drawers and doodahs are all so extremely clever. Not because it's my instrument of…well, I suppose you'd call it *revenge*.

Fuck. My heart just raced like a train there. *Breathe, breathe.* I'm so out of my depth but there's no going back now. Is there?

Isabel's still fiddling with that knob, tugging at it now but it won't pull. She needs to—yeah, like that—by accident more than design, her fingers have fumbled it anticlockwise. With a satisfying click, an octagonal panel slides aside.

"Yes!" Isabel exclaims with delight, poking a finger into the cavity and scooping out three irregularly cut pieces of paper. They each have one side that is blank, fragments of some murky picture on the other. "Jigsaw pieces?" she says.

I make myself lean over her shoulder and feign surprise. "How strange," I say. "Seems this old thing is full of revelations."

She kindles a weird little smile as she lays the pieces out on the cup-ringed coffee table. I can almost hear the cogs whirring as she slides the scraps around. And, finally, she makes her move.

"How long have you known, Nora?"

I don't know what reaction I was expecting when this moment came. Guilt? Contrition, even? Maybe. Definitely not this smug twinkle in her eyes as she finally twigs that she's got a challenge on her hands. Although, yeah, the challenge isn't what she thinks it is. I'm not going to be fighting her, especially not over Marcie.

I sense she's expecting something waspish in reply, but I just say: "Long enough." I down my wine, pour myself another and put the bottle on the floor next to the couch. "You'll want to find the rest of those pieces." I let myself sink into the cushions, but the tension doesn't go. It just gets redistributed from my spine to my face. My jaw, so wired, it feels like I'm pulling a rictus instead of any kind of natural expression.

If Isabel notices, it doesn't put her off playing along now she knows what the game is. She gets busy around the chest. Probing, prodding, twisting, turning. A quarter rotation of the top opens up a shallow tray. Three more pieces. A hidden door at the back of a fully extended drawer. Five more pieces. The picture is still obscure but she's building an edge now. There's what looks like the interior corner of something and, maybe, an ear? At least it does to me, but then I know what the whole picture looks like. I could show it to her on my phone now but, if there's one thing I know about puzzlers, it's that they hate to be told the answer before they've worked it out. If there's another thing, it's that they always think they're the smartest person in the room. So... no. I'm so tired of this shit, but if I don't see it through to the end, I won't win. And I *really* want to win. I'm so sick of losing.

"So, where *is* Marcie, anyway?"

God knows why she's chosen now to address the stinking, cheating elephant in the room. Is she laying her cards on the table in some sort of a power move? Clearing away the opening pawns to jump us closer to the endgame? Fucked if I know. I think I'm supposed to respond with something smart like, *oh, she's around here somewhere* or *you know she really threw herself into solving that thing*, but this is my home, so we're playing by my rules.

So, I say, "It's just the two of us tonight, I'm afraid."

Which, considering the time that's elapsed since I called her, printed out the picture, cut the pieces up and distributed them about the chest's easier accessed areas could theoretically be true by now.

Isabel is working quickly. She's discovered by stretching her arms right around it that some of the chest's mechanisms have to be operated simultaneously. Still others need to be triggered in sequence. Things are popping, sliding, swinging open as the beast unfolds itself to her. I just let her get on with it, scrolling Facebook, scowling at a friend's engagement announcement and getting drunk as quickly as possible. Occasionally, I hear little moans of frustration, tight little yips of triumph.

Then: "What the actual fuck?"

And: "What is this, Nora? Some sort of sick joke?"

And, shouting now: "Where's Marcie? Marcie! Come out, you bitch!"

Marcie doesn't, to my knowledge, reply but now does seem to be the time to kick things up a level.

"Oh, I don't think she can come out, Isabel." I rise unsteadily from the couch. "You might be able to free her if you can work out how to open it all the way up, but you'll need to be quick. All those drawers and doors fit very snugly. There can't be a lot of air getting in there."

The looks she gives me then. There's fleeting shock, then a moment of pure fear that quickly crystalises into outrage. I mean, I get it. Imagine being outwitted by me.

"Get her out," she seethes.

"Me?" I say with all the mock innocence I can muster. "I wouldn't know how to start. That…" I gesture at the clumsy, home-made jigsaw on the coffee table, "…was a work of genius of yer woman's own making. Her moment of triumph at completing the puzzle, but…" We both stare down at the image of my wife squashed inside the beast's belly like one of those ancient peat-bog people, a manoeuvre necessary to operate the mechanisms of the final puzzle. Her triumphant grin already collapsing as she realized that whatever she'd done had triggered the chest's speedy self-reassembly.

"Didn't you even try to free her, you moron?" Isabel says, though her sneer lacks conviction.

"Course I did," I reply. "But *my* poor wee brain isn't up to the task. Why do you think you're here?"

I can see that she's already moved on from that. Is working through the permutations.

She's thinking: *Fucking hell, get me an axe.*

She's thinking: *No, if Marcie could do this, I can bloody well do it faster.*

She says, "This can't be fucking real."

This is the moment, so I let it stretch and expand like the glorious bubble of shimmering, bitter joy that it is. Then I pop it by laughing in her deceitful face.

"Of course, it's not *real*, you utter roaster."

Isabel's eyes widen with a confusion of relief and rage. Her cheeks manage somehow to pale and pinken simultaneously. She's actually quite pretty when she's at a complete loss.

"Marcie's fine," I say. "I've banished her for the weekend to think about what she's done. Without her phone or laptop, in case you were wondering why she's not been in touch today. You really did take me for a mug, didn't you?"

"So how did you find out?" That supercilious smugness rising up again.

I snort. "Unlike a lot of people these days," I tell her, "I'm actually on very good terms with my neighbours and you're not *actually* invisible, you know. Round this manor, lipstick that colour tends to get remembered."

That shuts her up for a good few seconds.

"So, what now?" Isabel says at last.

"Well, I'd really like you to fuck off," I say, and there isn't an ounce of lie in *that* statement. "But…it might be to your advantage to complete the chest's puzzles. There's a memory card in there with some bits of video from…" I check my phone's calendar and reel off several specific dates and times, all of them when I'd been working or up at the home visiting Mum, or any of the other things a normal person does with their day.

A normal person might have offered an apology at this point but, all I get is: "So, they're not on the cloud?" Forever trying to calculate her options, which she can't do, because she can no longer think of me as dull, dowdy Nora. She doesn't know *what* I am any more.

I shake my head. "I'm old school and besides, that wouldn't be sporting. If you can find the card, it's done with. If not…" I smile, "… I'm sure I'll work out how to upload them eventually. It's up to you."

The relief I feel when I turn my back on her and leave the room, closing the door behind me, is indescribable. But once that initial rush is over, I realize that winning doesn't feel that good after all. The yawning, sucking hole inside me that's been there since I was cheated out of my happiness, modest as it was, is still there. Fuck, or maybe I'm just hungry.

As I busy myself around the kitchen, slicing bread and beating eggs for the French toast that will keep me going until it's time for my planned pizza and Shudder session, I keep half an ear open for the door. But I don't expect to hear it and, in the end, stop listening, leaving Uncle Henry's magical chest to do its work. Beautiful, old, inexplicable beast, that it is.

It's when I'm squeezing out the ketchup that it occurs to me to wonder: What does it do with the bodies?

HUNGER

ELIANE BOEY

IT'S the scents that rouse you; the gamey fat of roast duck, and the warm syrup of the dragon fruit and mandarins under the red lamps. You shrink at the acrid musk of incense, from the habits of a life that doesn't feel like it was ever yours. But the smoke has always been a connection between those who extend the invitation, and those who wait to be let in. A language you never knew you understood. The smoke fingers the air, and finds you.

The gates between the worlds are open.

You don't recognize this part of Chinatown. Nothing is allowed to age in Singapore, but it has only been a year. In your grandfather's time, Sago Lane was called Dead Man's Lane by the Hokkien, after the houses of death that lined the street, where the poorest came to hide their wasted flesh in the mean cubicles on the upper floors, and await the end. Death upstairs and rites downstairs, all across the road from the affluent homes and clan houses.

As you walk, pairs of hollowed eyes look up at you, from where they squat along the five-foot-way. Gorging on platters of steamed cakes, tea, and whole fruit. It isn't their first time returning. Do they eat because it fills them, or because they hunger? Now you know it isn't the street that has changed. The ones that came before you beckon you to join them, but you bow hurriedly, and move on. It has only been a year since you crossed the gates.

Since you belonged with the dead.

～

Where Ann Siang Hill curves into Club Street, a burn barrel smoulders with the curling ash of the yellow prayer paper that the living set alight on the seventh month, to signify the opening of the gates. The shophouses on this part of the street are painted in bright colours, for their new lives as cocktail bars and restaurants. The street is as it was since you were part of the crowd that filled it. Except the lively invitations, of the young people draped on the refurbished terraces, calling out to friends on the street, are not meant for you.

You wished you stayed behind when the gates opened. Except it wasn't the incense that called, and the scents, but the hunger.

The teak double doors of the clan house at the top of the hill are open, although a carved screen has been erected between the threshold and the interior. It's a Cantonese trader's association founded before the nation knew its name; uneasy neighbours with the bars and restaurants that now dwell in the converted shophouses painted in neon colours. The five-foot-way in front of the house is veiled in its own blend of incense, and the oil of rosewood furniture warmed under wrinkled palms. You smell damp tea leaves, newsprint ink, and the sweet deception of cloves in kretek cigarettes. There is something else, underneath the heady smoke, which draws you. It's the nutty, rich fat of a roast duck, which sits on a table just before the threshold. Lean forward, and the scent awakens your hunger.

That's when you see *them*, staring. They're sat at round tables on the road that is closed to traffic this time of night. The tables are covered with pink plastic, and littered with melon seed, peanut shells, and half-empty cups of tea. Behind the tables, a low stage with its sides of raw wood on bare steel bars still visible. You take a step back, and the ones who squat to eat by the side of the road laugh at your fear. They remind you that all of this is for you, at the annual opening of the gates. When the lights come on and the singing begins, they rise, and drag leaden feet towards the chairs nearest the stage. But the blinding light, the loud music, and the garish mansions, cars, stacks of hell notes, and dolls in bright coloured paper, only remind you of what they are not, and the things you lost.

Nothing prepared you for finding yourself on the other side of the gates. Waiting between two worlds to be let in, but only on the month of the Hungry Ghost Festival. Nose trained for the first tendrils of smoke and sweet fat. You never depended on anyone the way you do now, when you were among the living. You certainly never feared their presence. On the first opening of the gates, you thought of how you missed the outside, and the streets that do not recognize you. How you miss the food.

Oh, the food is the reward for the year's wait.

That was before you sat at the first table you came upon, only to find you could not eat, because of the way they looked at you, daring themselves to feel as they believe. Knowing that their invitation came only from tradition. Of fear at the threads between the worlds broken, and their protection lost with it, if they stopped. You saw the fear and disbelief you once had. And so, you turned away from the table of food, your belly empty. How could you eat of their spread, when you still see yourself as they do?

Perhaps next year you'll try to stay behind. But you already know that next year, the hunger will command. The ones who came before you say that offerings used to be plentiful throughout the year. Now the tables are open and incense burned on the seventh month. That is why, by the opening of the gates, all who waited are famished.

It's another night, and you're back. You're still hungry. You passed laden tables on the way to Club Street, but you ignored them, because it has to be the roast duck in front of the clan house. Hunger is a toothed worm that bores a hole in you. Each night that you do not eat, it masticates the parts of you that still feel. Tonight, you walked with the crowds on North Bridge Road, although you hated how you folded yourself away from their paths, and avoided their glances. You hated how all the while you wondered if they even felt or saw you at all. And that you still do not know if they did.

You're at the top of Ann Siang Hill, and the table is full again, as it was the night before. This time, none of them are looking. They're sat at the tables, all except for the front row, which you already know is intended for you. Their eyes are on the stage, as the lights train their focus on a woman in early middle age, bold sequins and vinyl boots. She taps the microphone near her ear. There is still time for you to eat. You step towards the table.

The screech of the microphone through a loudspeaker tears your face open.

When you think how it was when you were one of them, you're certain that you never felt this hungry. That hunger did not drive you as it does now. It never *haunted* you, and drove you to walk the length of North and South Bridge Roads, where all you saw were eyes. The offering of food and incense is a poor trade, annual gifts to keep your worlds apart, until the next opening. Yet even with the gates open, their unseeing stares are a wall that you cannot pass. There's a clinking sound behind you, and before you can turn, a grey cat springs to the table. Its claws rend lines on the yellow cloth. The cat has upset the platter of steamed cakes in landing, but it pays it no mind. It lunges for the duck, and your mouth waters as though you would taste it too. But the cat hisses and arches its back, and the men at the nearest table turn to look.

From where you stand in the quiet shadow, you see that the skin on the roast duck has swelled on the slow-cooling damp of its heat, and is no longer crisp. But the lush scent of the fat between skin and meat drifts on the slight breeze, and touches the inner curl of your nostril. You see yourself at the table, ignoring the rice, the cold tea, and the boiled sweets that have been left out since the afternoon, their fluorescent insides seeped through the wrappers and solidified in a swirl on the red plate. Only the meat will satisfy the year's hunger.

You ate today. You smelled the incense and felt the hunger, not in your stomach, but deep in the hollow of your chest. The table was set in front of a red altar in the back lane where two storied rows of shophouses on Emerald Hill meet in the shade of bougainvillea groaning with magenta flowers. It's a secluded path a minute away from the glare of Somerset and Orchard Road. There were two white styrofoam boxes of boiled chicken on greasy rice, and a pile of yellow steamed cakes on the table. Someone has stuck unburnt joss sticks in the cakes in the centre, and they stood like the skeletons of forgotten birthdays. The sticks in the small bronze tripod urn had burnt to stubs, held up by their own ash.

You crouched low, and saw the cold, pimpled skin of the chicken, and underneath, gelatine congealed on flesh. But hunger is a bony hand tapping a claw on your chest, and you must answer. And at least here, you are alone. You dug into the dry cakes in the glow of the pink light from a plastic lamp in the shape of a lotus. It's the meat you want, but the cakes you could swallow, unseen in the shadow of the bougainvillea. They tasted of grudging reunions, the arch of your mother's brow, and missed dinners at the office.

It was when you finished, and you looked up, that you saw them through the half-open kitchen door. A woman who appeared not far from the gates herself, on a sofa beside a man with the dull and ageless face of one no longer young because nothing interests them anymore. A Mandarin language variety show on a handsome, flat-screened TV is the only light in their eyes. You tell yourself that you do not know them, although you recognized everything in that large, comfortable, cold living room.

Still, hunger taps another bony finger on your ribs.

On the closed-off road outside the clan house, the *ge tai* performance is at its giddy peak. Bright costumes, light like sharpened knives, and earnest Hokkien songs reverberating through speakers which compete with the music streaming from the bars. As it is every night, the front row of seats is empty, and the table is full yet again. The ones who came before are wetting parched lips on the fat of the roast. They see you, and do not beckon this time, but leave space at the table. But you can no more stand their welcome than the cool invitation of those who laid the spread. And that's enough to make you leave. Except, the hunger no longer knocks on your bones now, it crushes them.

There's something else tugging on the loose seams of your mind, and it's a full minute before you realize; that you know this song. It's all there. The rhythmic click of the cha cha beat. And the song—about the small pleasures of a hard life—that was the soundtrack of your childhood. Of drowsy afternoons at Popo's flat, after school. Watching cartoons on her boxy Toshiba TV, while she prepared double-boiled soup and steamed fish for dinner. A roast duck leg from the Cantonese coffeeshop, if it was a birthday. Now, you don't wonder that the songs performed at *ge tai* have not changed in decades, nor that everything behind the gates both repels you and intensifies your hunger.

Laughing, you widen your jaw. You don't see the ones that came before. You don't see those who laid the feast because it was their duty, now clapping their hands, whistling, and enjoying the performance they stage every seventh month, for you. Your tongue extends from between moist teeth. It touches the roast duck, and you lick. And bite, into the skin. The skin is still crisp. You feel the resistance, and the snap. Then you let the jus and oil pour down your chin. Now, the hunger is gone.

REPETITIONS

TIM COOKE

I PUT the book flat on the kitchen table and sipped my coffee. The noise of her pencil scratching the paper, as she coloured in part of a detailed forest scene, was interrupted only by the birds on the feeders outside. I looked through the French doors at the plum tree, from which the basket of nuts and the tube of Nyjer seeds hung. They teemed with activity: chaffinches, coal tits, blue tits, a nuthatch and more, flitting between the branches. It was not yet lunch time and I'd already seen the crossbills and our resident woodpecker—the benefits of this slowly-crumbling hill farm in mid-Wales. In the distance, above the scorched patchwork valley, swooped a red kite, so commonplace it was hardly worth noting.

Look at the kite up there, love. She placed her pencil perpendicular to the page and followed the direction of my finger. *Do you remember how to identify it?* She pursed her lips and tapped her chin, pretending to think.

Oh yeah, the forked tail.

Well done. I ruffled her thickly-knotted hair and got to my feet, then stepped towards the window. There was something else—smaller, with broader wings—circling the woodland beyond the green lane. *Ah, now what's that?* Her curiosity piqued by the genuine tone of my question, she fetched the binoculars from the sill and handed them to me.

What do you think it is?

I fixed my gaze on the soaring bird and lifted the lenses to my eyes, but I'd missed it. I scanned the landscape, sliding left over the newly-ploughed fields and shining transmission towers. Just as a train rolled into view, a dull thud, both soft and hard, sprang from the window-pane and filled the room.

What was that? I turned to face her, but she had looped behind me and was already at the glass, peering through.

A sparrow, I think. It's hurt.

I moved over to her and leaned forward.

It's a wren, love.

We watched as it twisted onto its side, one wing caught beneath it, the other projecting upwards, flapping without method. It toppled onto its back and kicked its legs into the air, then fell still. The only persisting movement was the rapid in-out motion of its tiny speckled breast.

What can we do, Dad? Is it dead?

I think it's stunned. Find me a box from the recycling. She came back with one from the brewery and I told her to punch holes in the top with a skewer, while I searched for a tea towel in the bottom drawer.

Is this enough?

More than that, love. I took the tool from her and stabbed repeatedly across the two flaps on the top. I handed the box back and we walked together to the utility room and through the back door. We strode around the side of the house, pools of hot sun and cool shade, and came to the bird. It looked stiff—the chest wasn't moving anymore. I bent down, getting as close as I could, and saw that it was, in fact, still breathing. Its beak was open. I imagined its breath warm against my skin.

It's alive, isn't it, Dad?

It sure is.

Are we going to make it better?

We can try.

With the tea towel draped over my hand, I fumbled gently with the squat bird. I couldn't get any purchase on it—there was so little of it to grip, it kept slipping through my gloved fingers, as if coated in oil. Changing tack, I managed to roll it with my right hand into the palm of my left and fold the towel around it.

Open the box, love. I placed the wren inside and lifted as much of the material away from it as I could, then fixed the top shut. *We'll put it round by the hose and check in half an hour.*

Back inside, she continued with her colouring, while I made lunch. I fetched a tin of beans from the pantry, poured its contents into a pan and put them on to boil. The rack was empty, so I checked the draining board by the sink for the bread knife and found it unwashed in the basin. I rinsed the serrated blade, then took the loaf from the paper bag on the side, sawed off two slices and put them under the grill.

Do you want cheese with yours?

She tapped her chin again.

No thanks.

Get the sauce and the cutlery then, please.

Okay.

Once I'd scraped the last of the beans onto the toast, I took the plates to the table and sat down opposite her. She tilted her head sideways and began cutting her meal into squares. Helping myself to mine, I watched as she used two hands to squeeze a blob of ketchup onto a clear section of the porcelain, trying at once to brush hair from her eyes with her wrist. She felt my gaze and glanced up.

Do you need help, love?

I'm fine thanks. She put the bottle down and started to eat. *Did you look like me when you were young, Dad?* she asked, through a mouthful of food.

Yes, a lot. Except for the hair. You've got your mother's hair. Mine was much lighter—bright blond.

Was it long, like mine?

No. My fringe stopped here. I lifted my hand horizontally to my eyebrows. *It was this length all the way round.*

Oh.

Yes, but your mouth and eyes are the spitting image.

What does that mean?

Exactly the same.

That's nice. She looked back down. *How do you think the wren's doing?*

Finish up and we'll check.

She pushed a soggy crust towards the rim.

I'll be sad if it's dead already, she said, frowning. I lowered my fork, catching a beam of light from the window and causing her to wince.

She continued, *I don't want it to die, but if it's going to, I want to see it. I've seen dead things before, but I've never watched anything die. Have you?*

I thought involuntarily of the room above us: smooth sheets, dust, wooden chairs for bedside tables, two brass lamps and a broken cabinet; the stench of lavender. I closed that door and delved further back, into my own childhood. It didn't take long.

Yes, I have. Let's check the bird first and I'll tell you about it.

The cardboard flaps scraped too loudly as I slid them apart. I stopped, waiting on a commotion from the interior. Nothing happened and my hope faded. I made the gap wide enough for us both to see in, and it quickly became apparent that the wren was, in fact, still alive. It stood completely still, glistening like a bronze sculpture on a piece of the now shit-stained material. She leaned forward, blocking my view, and exhaled.

It's getting better, isn't it? Her left hand, which was pressed against the stone wall for support, turned pink. I looked at the freckle on the webbing between her thumb and index finger. It had been there since she was two and I'd used it to teach her how to tell left from right.

Yes, it's doing well. It's still stunned, though. We should give it another half hour.

I sent her to fill a small terracotta pot with water, while I went to the barn for a cup of sunflower seeds. The latch on the barn door was boiling. I lifted it and squeezed my fingers between the oak panels, pulling them open. This was the oldest part of the farm, the most weathered; I liked it the least. Inside, the air was thick with chemicals: diesel, pesticides and chlorine. The wood stacked below the wool loft would need replenishing soon. I found the bag of seeds at the foot of the chest freezer, but no cup. I reached in and recoiled, remembering that I had not resealed it since the last time. I steadied myself with the usual question—What's the worst can happen?—and tried again.

Both fists full, I crossed the paving stones, past the foxgloves curving over the garden wall—sentries armed to the teeth—and rounded the corner. She was down on her knees, hands inside the box. I started to jog.

What are you doing?

She looked up, mouth ajar.

Just putting the water in. She lifted the pot balanced on her fingertips so I could see.

Ah, yes—carefully, then.

I knelt next to her and loosened my grip, letting the seeds stream into a small mound in the corner. I stood up and cast the rest over the patio, before fixing the top shut again.

~

Both elbows planted on the table, she drank her lemonade, leaving a moustache of bubbles above her lip, which she licked with exaggerated pleasure.

It was a crow, love—I'm not sure what kind. I rested my chin on my knuckles. *It wasn't long after your grandmother passed. I was nine or ten. I spent a lot of time in the garden and in the playing fields behind our house, which was on the edge of town. I remember finding a dead hedgehog by the football changing rooms and dissecting it over a few days—I wanted to be a vet, you see.* This wasn't true.

What's dissected?

It means to cut open and have a look. Anyway, I was desperate for a pet back then, but your grandfather wouldn't allow it. He was busy working and didn't like animals. He didn't want to clean up more than he had to. I looked at the piles of washing up in the sink and on the draining board, lunch plates still on the table. *So I decided to catch a bird and raise it myself in secret. I set a trap on the lawn, below the beech trees. It wasn't very good— just a toy shopping basket held up on one side by a couple of twigs. I put some grapes underneath and watched from a distance. I didn't think for a second it would work, but I waited all afternoon. I needed the toilet so badly, but I didn't move, in case I missed it.* She wiped at another moustache. *Then, out of the blue, the crow landed. It hopped a few paces and that was that, I had my own bird.*

What did you do with it?

I slid a piece of cardboard between the grass and the basket, so it couldn't escape, then carried it to the shed. I kept it there for a few days—out of the cage of course—and took it food and water. But something wasn't right—it wasn't meant to be shut in like that. On the third or fourth morning, I pushed the door open and found it dragging itself across the floor, unable to fly or even stand. I tried to get it to drink, but it wouldn't. I took it onto the lawn and set it free, but it just lay there, shaking. I stayed with it for the afternoon and into the evening. Finally, it stopped breathing and I buried it by the fence. I felt awful about it, terrible. I couldn't sleep. I never did anything like that again.

Did you tell Grandad?

I shifted in my seat and sighed.

He knew about it. He'd been watching from an upstairs window.

Did he help you feel better?

No, love, he didn't. But that's another story. Shall we go and check on our friend?

She downed the last of her drink and smiled, shuffling her chair away from the table.

Yep, let's go.

She took my hand and we walked together to the utility room and pushed through the back door. We strode around the side of the house, pools of hot sun and cool shade, and came to the box. I opened the top, so we could both see. Perched on the rim of the terracotta bowl, its barred tail flicking in and out of the water, the wren stared at us, full of life.

I think it's ready to go, love.

She wrapped her arms around my waist and pressed herself firmly into my torso.

We put the box on the wall, flaps wide apart, and stepped back to watch. The noise of a tractor rumbled from the next farm and I smelled a bonfire. Almost immediately, the bird scrambled from its enclosure and took flight, undulating low across the field into the pine trees beyond the lane. For the first time all day, I felt a rush of wind.

And that's that, she said, before setting off towards the barn.

I clicked the switch on the kettle and took the novel from the table. The sun had dipped now and streamed through the French doors, heat filling the kitchen. I lay on the sofa facing out over the valley and read a paragraph. My eyelids grew heavy, so I put the book down on my chest and let myself drift towards sleep. I listened as she played her imaginative game between the grass and the patio. She called to the wren—and to other birds, too. I remembered my crow: two-legged hops, the falling basket casting shadows deep and wide. I watched it turn circles on the lawn, in full view of the darkness swelling at the top of the house.

I woke to a thud and a crack, a small face ricocheting away from the glass. The features—much like my own—creased into a familiar frown. A spurt of blood spilled from a crevice in the brow, running in thick lines down the chin.

I swung my feet onto the floor, launched myself across the kitchen and charged, heart thumping, through the utility room. I raced around the patio and found the body slumped on the ground, legs straight and torso curved forward. The blood dripping from the head pooled in a gap between the flagstones. I grabbed the towel from the box on the wall and covered the wound, struggling to lift the limp form into my arms.

It's okay, love, I'm here—you're fine. Oh my god. Let's go inside and have a proper look.

I carried the weight through the hall and up the stairs, legs trembling. I stumbled across the landing into the bathroom, where I sat with the child cradled in my lap. Using the towel, I tried to wipe the blood away but smeared bird shit along the jawline.

It's not so bad, love—just a big old bang. Fucking hell.

I heard footsteps and glanced up; there was nothing there. I rubbed at the earthy stain on the skin with my thumb, noticing my own freckle that I'd used to learn left and right. There was a loud creak—the sixth step—and the patter of shoes on wood. I looked up again, hardly able to breathe. She rounded the corner and stopped in the doorframe, mouth ajar.

Is everything okay, Dad?

Her face was clear, flushed with summer play and worry. I looked down at the child in my arms, the mop of light blond hair matted with dried clots, fringe plastered to his forehead.

Why are you sitting like that?

I shut my eyes and opened them again. My hands were empty now, clutching at dead air.

You look like you've seen a ghost.

LULLABY FOR THE UNSEEN

NELLY GERALDINE GARCÍA-ROSAS

1.

I DID NOT WANT to see a corpse. But I *did* want to.

So when mama said *Don't look* as we approached the crowd, I squeezed my eyes shut until I saw sparks.

Although I must have watched a little when my eyelids got tired. And it does not count if it is only a tiny glimpse, a sneak peek at the *how could this happen* and the *oh my lord and lady and all the saints*, a glance of the *but it was merely a child, only a monster would do something like this.*

2.

There is a house that sits in the corner of two busy streets. It has a dirty coat of smog, mold, spit and piss. The once off-white walls are peeling, showing the house's past lives when it was teal, bright yellow, maybe coppery orange. But barely anyone notices the house itself. People lean on its grimy walls not knowing—not wanting to know—someone lives there, perhaps no one does. This corner is used as an improvised bus stop because one day someone made the stop sign with their arm and the bus stopped and every other bus did too the next day and then the next, and they kept on stopping and people noticed. And when people notice something, things happen.

3.

Ariel. It is because of him that I have this scar.

He was my classmate. A very thin kid, shorter than me, with greasy black hair and sunken eyes that showed dark bags under them, maybe bruises, I do not know. He never cut his nails so the teachers reprimanded him constantly for that; until they grew tired, or stopped caring. He loved playing on the floor, I believe he did, because his school pants were soiled and had been patched several times.

4.

On the house that no one notices' east side corner, steel grille adorns frosted glass panes showing that there were art deco pretensions in the early stages of construction of this brutalist-by-force building. The windows abruptly turn medieval as they approach the house next door, merely resembling arrowslits. If there was an attentive enough passerby, they would spot only one thing, though, the tinted-glass inverted crosses on the other side of the house.

5.

When I opened my Spanish notebook, I was greeted by Ariel's handwriting: *u like looking at kreepy stuff, don't u? i'll show u something kool.*

I wanted to see, so I called mama and told her that I would be doing an assignment with my classmates after school, and that one of them would walk me home later in the afternoon.

6.

I'm telling you there are people in that house. I think they're people. Some say they're brujos. They keep duendes or some other small creature in that hideous place and charge fifty pesos to let you see them—or feel them—because the interior is pitch dark. Just before your eyes get used to the darkness, you hear tiny footsteps approaching and then something *runs around and between your legs, scratching your skin, breathing warmly against it.*

7.

Someone spread quicklime at the bus stop where the body had lain before. A couple of praying candles already burned out left smoke trails on the dirty wall.

Ariel said that the cool thing he wanted to show me was not on the street, but in his house. Inside, it reeked of rotten fruit and candle wax.

8.

A visitor who were to enter the house would notice that its door is comprised of three layers. A filigree wrought iron frame delicately covers ripple textured glass like in Spanish style buildings. But in the interior, a metal plate is carelessly soldered to the doorframe as a quick privacy measure or a way to not let light in.

9.

The dolls were carefully placed on an old sofa. Ariel said we could not touch them, only look. There must have been two dozen, maybe more. Unlike other dolls, their skin looked grey and wrinkly like old leather, their clothes were soiled. They all had bright eyes and long eyelashes, like the Christ child.

There are dolls that are not to be played with mama said one time in church when I asked about the ivory boy that was inside a bell jar.

10.

Similar to other local buildings, the house has an interior courtyard where a tejocote tree grows. Unlike those colonial houses, this space was not planned or intended, it came to be when a ceiling collapsed after an earthquake and was never rebuilt. Some of the rubble remains there because the inhabitants of the house refuse to take it out.

11.

We played in the inner courtyard where there are stairs that do not go anywhere. From the top, I could see a small house made out of rubble. Ariel told me it was the dolls' house and I laughed because an ugly house was perfect for his ugly dolls. I said that, contrary to what he promised, they were not cool at all. He pushed me down the dilapidated stairs.

My eyebrow needed six stitches. Mama said I was lucky I did not lose an eye. She did not say anything about me lying to her, but I know she is disappointed in me. She will not let me play near Ariel's house anymore.

12.

Sleep, my little one.
The boy's inside the house.
And he is very tiny.
And he has broken bones.
Hushaby, my love.
The house is full of shadows.
And you seek praying candles.
And you hear praying songs.
Sleep, my little one.
The darkness is inside.
And you heard him approaching.
And you will feel his hands.
Hushaby, my love.
The boy has long, long nails.
And he walks in the shadows.
And he is very dead.

13.

A girl goes to that house alone, but no one notices her. No one sees her ringing the doorbell that sounds like a muffled buzzing coming from inside. Only she hears quick, small footsteps, like a child's. But no one comes to answer. She rings again, and again she hears the buzzing and the footsteps that sound like moving away this time. She waits, but no one answers. She knocks on the metallic doorframe with a coin, then puts her ear close just to hear the footsteps further away. Yet she feels someone on the other side of the door listening, waiting, breathing heavily. She knocks again and says she's one of Ariel's friends from school who came here to forgive him. To ask him to forgive her. She apologizes for being so insistent right now, but she feels bad for what happened, for what she said that day. But she now has an answer to his question: She does, she loves looking at things she should not.

I saw your dead body that day on the floor, Ariel. I want to see you again.

No one notices that she slips a sheet of paper under the door. Her tight handwriting in sparkling purple ink. She apologizes again, but she thinks she should go home and stop bothering. Yet she stays to hear the rustling of paper. And the breathing on the other side sounds stronger and the small footsteps come closer and a metallic click reverberates.

And the door opens.

THE TUMOUR ROOM

ALEXANDER JAMES

I DIDN'T EXPECT to see David again. Some part of me believed he was still trapped in that room, waiting for me to return. And that part was right.

~

My bus home broke down in that space you find between towns. Wastelands of failing dealerships and shuttered warehouses, a grubby patchwork of nowheres. The driver shook me from my half-cut slumber, dispelling those fitful and protean dreams I'd hoped the drink would banish. Myself and the few other passengers onboard were hustled off into the deserted street to wait under a too-small shelter. It would be at least another forty minutes until a replacement service would get to us. A weak but insistent patter of rain blew in across my shoulders, and as I began to sober up I felt the chill seeping through my coat. Down the road I could see the glow of a caff, some measure of warmth promised in the LED coffee cup that twinkled on and off behind the steamed-up windows. Perfect, I thought. I could get a warm drink, text my wife. Clear my head.

A scene drab and tired even by the standards of the area greeted me. Pensioners from a nearby estate sat scattered around in ones and twos, staring off into space with rheumy eyes or mumbling to themselves over empty, smeared plates. The faint odour of stale smoke clung to the yellowing pine panels, and the formica tables were topped with what was either a mineral pattern or flecks of old stains too stubborn to shift. Up in one corner a TV buzzed with some news show, brightness turned up to the point where it was impossible to tell what the hosts were discussing, reduced as they were to a pair of mannequins with black holes for mouths.

Eventually the owner appeared at the counter, an unhealthy-looking man in his sixties. I asked for a cup of tea and he grunted and waddled off back into the kitchen. Turning and scanning the room for a secluded table, it was only at that moment that I noticed him. He was parked by the translucent glass, a near-empty Styrofoam cup in his hands. David. Older, yes. Older than his years, judging from the hollowness to his face, the bones shifting in his knuckles. But you show me the boy and I'll show you the man.

He hadn't seen me, I realized. There was still time to leave, to brave the cold and the dark outside rather than whatever this encounter would bring. But as I deliberated, frozen with indecision, he felt my gaze upon him and turned to meet it.

"Hello, stranger," I managed to say.

His face twisted up for a split-second before he recognized me. "Evan!"

As he got up and strode over he broke into a tobacco-stained smile. "It's been too long. Far too long, pal."

"Yeah. How have you been?" I tried to match his smile with my own inane grin.

"You know. Same old, same old," he said.

I nodded, but I had no idea what he meant by that. Not really. It had been decades, after all.

A missed beat passed between us.

"How have you been?" I managed to repeat.

"Yeah. Alright. Been better." His voice was harsh, like he'd been smoking a pack a day since we last met. "You were on that bus?"

"Mm. Replacement should be here soon enough."

"Maybe. I doubt anyone's in a hurry to come down these ends." He thumbed at the decrepit scene outside, reduced to a merciful blur. "Rent's cheap, mind you."

"Didn't know you lived around here."

His smile faltered for a second. "Yeah. I move around a lot, these days." He coughed. "Yourself? Thought a fella like you would've gotten out of the area altogether."

"I'm just...passing through."

"Oh."

He looked like he was about to say something more, but he stopped himself. "Come on. Sit with me."

As I did, I wondered if anyone else recognized David in there. Probably not. A long time had passed since his spell in the public consciousness.

We stuck to the safe topics. How our mums were doing. Funny things that'd once happened at school. Endless afternoons together, hours spent exploring the hidden corners of our world. I almost enjoyed it at first, but it quickly became hard work. After a while his responses grew muted and clipped, statements of fact and little else, and his eyes seemed to film over. I resisted the urge to peel back my cuff and catch a glimpse of my watch.

Eventually the lulls between my questions and his listless replies grew too long to bear, and I must admit my curiosity got the better of me.

"Are you still in touch with Ed and Lewis, then?" I asked, trying to sound offhand.

He shrugged. "Last thing I'd heard, Ed was missing and Lewis had OD'ed."

"Jesus."

He shrugged again, as if it were no great surprise. We sat in silence for a minute. The owner came and dropped before me tea the colour of a pothole puddle.

"Really, though? I can't believe it. They were...alright. Back then. They seemed alright to me. Weren't they?"

"Yeah. Do you remember my old place?" he asked suddenly, his eyes shifting back to me.

"Of course. Nice street. And that old canal out back. Surprised we didn't get tetanus."

"I mean the house, though." David's stare didn't falter. He was waiting for me to say it. *I* was waiting for me to say it.

"Ah. Yep. I remember the.... The, uh, the—"

"The tumour room." He finished for me.

"That's right," I said, clicking my fingers as if he were jogging my memory. "That's...that's what we called it."

I took a deep breath. "I've got to be honest," I tried to keep my voice light, to stop my foot from tapping away beneath the table. "That game we played in there. Well, it scared the shit out of me. Royally."

His brow creased, but then he laughed. And I laughed too. In fact, once I began it was difficult to stop. We must have looked a scene sat in that shabby caff, both cackling like lunatics until we cried. Even the old codgers on the other tables started to get a bit perturbed.

"Really," I continued, wiping my tears with the back of my hand. "I'm laughing, now, but...at the time. Ooh, boy. Kids and their imaginations, eh? It really stuck with me."

A twitch played across his lips. "Yeah. It stuck with me, too."

And that's when I knew he hadn't forgotten a thing.

David and I were never meant to be friends. Never meant to meet at all. My parents, a pair of downwardly-mobile career academics, were seeking a cheap and quiet place to write their papers while they waited for more senior colleagues to shuffle off the mortal coil and free up their posts. They settled far from their usual leafy orbit of London's suburbs to an area that you could call, if you were extremely charitable, 'up-and-coming.' I'd call it a hole, but maybe I'm biased. The local state school was the only option for me at that age, and they figured a year or two there was a price they were willing to pay. There'd be no lasting damage, they must've thought, nothing a return to the capital later wouldn't fix.

Despite their assurances, it was safe to say I didn't fit in from the off. An overly precocious boy with a cut-glass accent and a faint stammer was never going to get along with bored estate kids, and they quickly sussed out that I was made of softer stuff. After a couple of painful days milling around the edge of the playground, desperately seeking out a group I could join without getting shoved or worse, David came over and asked me if I wanted to play with him. Not football, he assured me. Make-believe games.

We spent all our time together after that. I wasn't sure why he took a shine to me. He must've been a kind of outcast too, although I could never quite figure out why. He wasn't outwardly different from the rest of the local boys, yet they gave him a wide berth all the same. At the very least, the more overt bullying stopped once I began hanging out with him, and the prospect of wiling away my sentence there until my parents stepped into those dead men's shoes was no longer quite so intolerable.

After school he would show me around the local area, the rusted-over machines and stretches of forgotten wilderness behind the terraces, the lay-bys choked with rubble and damp sofas, the ditches lined with iridescent scum. Where an adult would have seen decline and degradation, we saw only an adventure, a vast intertwined playground of wreckage and vegetation where your ideas could run riot. Once we had thoroughly tired ourselves out pretending to be knights or spacemen or explorers among the wreckage, we'd return to his house. The difference from my own was striking. It was smaller, and the ceilings were much lower, and it always smelled strongly of dried flowers no matter which room you were in. We could do whatever we wanted until his mum got back—play video-games, make pillow forts, or try and start fires in the garden made from twigs and crisp packets.

Eventually David's mum would return from her job as a carer at the local old people's home. She'd whip up potato wedges and fish fingers for us, and we would eat in front of the TV with trays on our laps. It was a completely different world, a far cry from the staid and fussy household life I was used to. My mother was less than thrilled at our friendship. I could tell even then that she held a certain antipathy towards David's mum. Not based on anything in particular, mind you —being called a bigot would've been the worst thing my mother could imagine—but I could feel her bristle with disapproval whenever I talked about what we'd gotten up to that week. We weren't like them, she once told me, when I asked at the dinner table if we could get a TV in our house too. They did things differently. Not wrong, she was quick to say. Just...differently.

A month or so later, David handed me a note in class. That afternoon he wanted to show me and a few others something special. I turned up at his doorstep to find Ed and Lewis, David's other friends, were waiting there as well. I didn't enjoy hanging out with those two. They didn't speak much and they had a weird musty smell about them, like their clothes had gotten wet and never dried out properly. Sometimes

Ed had bruises on his arms. But David said they were nice to him, and it's not like I could afford to be fussy, anyway.

David opened the front door and, motioning us to be quiet, led us up the stairs to the landing. It was funny, but until he pointed it out, I'd never really noticed the faded door tucked between the bathroom and his bedroom. Unless you made an effort, a real, conscious effort, your eyes would skip right over it.

"Promise not to tell anyone." He said to us.

We nodded.

"I mean it." He had a look in his eyes I hadn't seen before. "Even if a grown-up asks you. Even your own mum. Anyone."

Behind the door lay an empty room, too small and crooked to fit much of anything inside. Of whatever purpose it had originally fulfilled there was no trace. A single bare bulb struggled to light the windowless walls, and from floor to ceiling it had been painted a colour I still can't quite describe. Hints of red, purple, brown and grey, mixed up but not fully blended together. The colours of a butcher's shop, of offal slowly oxidizing in steel trays. A faint smell, too. Petrol, maybe, or cat piss.

I asked David what it was. He shrugged.

"It's called the tumour room. I couldn't get in, before. When Dad was around."

"Tumour room?" I said.

He nodded, and no further explanation followed. My first thought was that the room was older than the rest of the house. My second was that it had been *transplanted*, somehow, into the building. Maybe because of the name. It didn't belong there. It didn't belong anywhere. That doesn't make sense, I know. But nothing about that time made much sense.

I'd assumed the mere existence of that room was what David had wanted to show us, but it was not. What happened within the room was the real secret, you see. To discover it, you only needed to stand inside, switch off the light and gently pull the door closed, making very sure the loose and rickety handle didn't slide out of place as you did so.

Then, within a couple of seconds, every single time, you would begin to scream.

David never told us how he first discovered that.

I told him it was a bad joke. Even after he went inside to prove it, I had my doubts. I'd never heard a real scream before, only ones in the movies we watched, and they definitely didn't sound like that. So hoarse. Even the haunted expression he wore as he stumbled out afterwards failed to convince me. The slower boys might have been fooled, I thought, but not me.

No, it was only when my turn came to venture inside that I learnt David was telling the truth. Not because I remember what happened. But because I forgot.

You see, your experience of the tumour room could not be recalled. Ever. No matter what mental preparations you went through, no matter how much you willed yourself to commit *something, anything,* to memory, the result every time was the same. The light would go out, the door would close, and the very next thing you'd be sprawled out on the landing, staring up at the spackled ceiling, your throat ragged and your face wet with tears. The other boys would gather around you and ask you what you had heard, or felt, or seen, already knowing that you would only shake your head in reply and only the ghosts of words would escape from your lips.

～

"That's how you remember it?" David asked. He rubbed his face, slowly, then took a deep, shuddering breath.

I nodded. There was still no sign of the bus. I wondered what he would do if I tried to leave.

He paused. "Alright. Fine. Fine. What do you think happened next?"

～

It became a ritual for the four of us. Most afternoons after school we would go to David's house and take turns to play the game, as we called it. Well. 'Game' was misleading. There were no rules to speak of. It certainly wasn't a test of courage or memory for whoever was inside, as both would fail you uniformly and without exception. Holding out seemed impossible, and you were left only with the faintest shadows flitting through your mind afterwards. Perhaps the real game was for those on the outside. We would all share a moment of savage joy as we tried to hold the door shut against the desperate scrabblings and hammerings from within, until we would at last grow weary or bored and let our captive burst free.

In hindsight, it sounds...sadistic. I know. And there were times I felt guilty, yes, especially if someone came out having wet themselves or something, but they were always alright after a moment or two. That look on their face never lasted long. And you knew not to poke fun, because your time was coming sooner or later. Who was to say how you would react once the door was closed on you?

Things carried on like that for quite a while. If you asked me if we were having fun, I couldn't tell you. Whatever novelty the experience possessed for me wore off rapidly. Probably the same was true for the other boys. Mostly, I kept going back because I wanted to hang out with David. He never seemed to get bored or frightened of the room. If anything, it energized him.

"Why don't we go exploring again?" I suggested to him one day, as we propped Lewis up against the landing wall. "Outside?"

"We're exploring right now," he replied.

I tried to see it how he must have seen it. A quest, plumbing the mysteries of that organ-coloured room in the heart of the house. There must be a greater meaning to it, I told myself. Something that would explain its presence here, some reason why it did what it did. Yet with every visit my questions multiplied, not helped by David's reticence to discuss the topic any further than who the next volunteer was to be.

"You said you weren't allowed in, before." I broached.

"My dad put a lock on the door. But when I asked him, he pretended he didn't know anything." David snorted, but he wouldn't look at me. "I know it was him though. Cause the lock went when he did."

All he was interested in was if I could remember my time inside. I didn't want to let him down. And so, after coming to, I would screw shut my eyes and try to imagine what had caused me such terror mere seconds ago. I would catch only a void, the afterimages of blood pumping through my eyelids.

I kept it a secret. We all did. The only difference is that people noticed when I started changing. My body was absorbing what my mind could not, keeping a ledger all of its own that I had no conscious access to. My sleep grew increasingly disturbed with every visit to David's house. My fear of the dark returned, and I grew to dread the moment I'd have to turn off my bedside lamp. Whenever I thought of the room, I felt a gnawing in the pit of my gut. Looking back, it wasn't anxiety as much as aversion, an instinctual pulling back from a brink.

Of course, I sensed something was wrong, even if I didn't want to admit it. It only became apparent to my parents after an incident at school. One of my usual tormentors tried scaring me in class, jumping out from behind a door, and upon his emergence I broke his nose without a second thought. The teacher had to pull me off him. Only a spotless record up to that point saved me from being excluded. My parents were at a loss to explain my sudden change in behaviour—I'd always been such a polite boy—but they suspected David had something to do with it. Until they could figure out what was going on with me, they warned, I wasn't to visit his house again.

When I told him the bad news at school the next day, he blinked slowly, and said nothing for a long while. Just when I was about to repeat myself, he said:

"I think I know what to do, now. One last time. But I need your help."

I considered refusing, or suggesting Ed or Lewis go in my stead. But I did not.

"Okay."

~

He refused to explain until we were back once more before that half-hidden door. We had crept out of school early. If we were quick, my parents would have no idea I'd paid a visit to him.

"I've always trusted you the most, Evan." He spoke. Up close, I could see how the whites of his eyes were threaded with red, and how the skin around his mouth was now chapped and wet. "The others don't know what it's like."

"What do you mean?"

"I've seen your face. When you get out. You're like me. You nearly remember. Nearly. Which is why I need you."

He held out a soft hand, palm indented with crescents from his nails. "We need to go in together."

I must have visibly balked at his suggestion, for he took a step back.

"What?" he said. "What?"

"I..."

"You don't want to?"

"No," I shook my head. "No, David. I really don't."

"It's the only way. I'm sure of it. Together...I think something different will happen. We can help remind each other."

"No."

"Please."

"I won't."

When he realized I wasn't going to go along with it, his mood soured. "You're scared." He practically spat the word.

"Yes," I admitted. "I think we should close it. Forget about it."

"You're going to grass me up."

"I won't. I swear. You can do what you want. But I want to stop."

"Just this one thing. Come on. Be a pal."

He grabbed me and we tussled for a while. It was the kind of fights kids have when they don't really want to hurt each other. Pulling and grabbing on each other's shirts, trying to knock the other one down.

At one point we disengaged and stood there, panting. "I don't want to fight," I said. David only shook his head.

Then he lunged at me and I felt the awful yawning of the tumour room at my back. With a strength borne of purest fear, before he could properly get hold of me again, I spun and shoved him over the threshold and into the unlit room. As he toppled, his hands shot out, one scrabbling purchase upon the inside handle of the door. It swung shut, hard. With a squeal and a clunk, the loose bolt inside the door-handle slid out and into that blackness with him. On my side, the brass knob dropped away, thudding uselessly to the carpet.

David began to scream. It was different, that time. Worse.

I don't think I'm an evil person. My whole life, I've never hurt anyone on purpose. But at that moment, I didn't stop it. Sure, I made some cursory effort to put the handle back in place, and then to barge down the door, which was far tougher than its flimsy appearance belied. But then...well, maybe I was scared of being found out. Or maybe, deep down, I wanted to know what would happen, and I'd rather it happened to him than to me.

I stumbled down the stairs, David's increasingly shrill cries following me out of the house, and I ran all the way back through the town. Upon reaching my family home, dishevelled from my headlong sprint, my mother asked me where I had been. I mumbled a mealy-mouthed excuse about forgetting my stuff at school and having to go back for it, and with that I sealed his fate.

David's mum should have found him after she finished her work. A half-hour later at most. How was I supposed to know she'd been called back in for an emergency? That she'd left a message for David on the answerphone telling him to go to his grandma's that night?

Much later, she called my parents, asking if he was there. And by then, it was too late to tell anyone.

Nobody questioned me much, afterwards, even though we were never seen without the other. My parents must have had their suspicions, but they didn't want to get us tangled up with the police or social services. The official verdict, I managed to piece together from their mutterings into the phone that weekend, was that David had been home alone and somehow had a seizure upstairs. Such things could manifest at any time. No mention of a strange little room, no evidence anyone else had been there with him.

"She was out, when it happened," my mother tutted down the line to some local gossip. "And she's supposed to be a nurse?"

I didn't see David at school again. Our teachers told us he'd gone to the hospital, and then a few weeks later, that he'd moved out of the area altogether. The other kids asked me what had happened, but I pleaded ignorance. They must have believed me, as I rapidly became a social nonentity again once the interest died down.

～

And that, for the longest time, was that. My parents switched me to a new school further away where things weren't quite so bad. I went to college after, got a job and stayed in the county while they moved away. It's strange, but it felt like home by then. I doubt I would've fitted back into London life anyway. They weren't too happy about it, but I've done alright without them.

A decade or so after he left, David's house, along with all the others on that street, were torn down with vague promises of redevelopment that never came to pass. The council probably didn't want the wrong kind of tourists coming to gawk at it, or even worse, pay respects. I wondered if the workmen had noticed anything when they smashed in the walls of that particular terrace, a curious difference in layout or proportions. Perhaps shards of the tumour room lay lodged beneath the mounds of scree and soil, some proof that it had once existed. That what had happened was real, or real enough.

～

David was quiet when I'd finished.

"That's how I remember it," I said, when the silence had grown taut. "All of it."

He ignored me.

"Four hours," he said, staring out into the night. "Four hours until someone found me. And I know what you're going to ask me next."

He looked back to me. "No. Nothing. Not a single fucking thing. It's like that time never existed to me."

I felt a curdled sting of disappointment, relief. Shame.

"Physically, it was a different story. Voice was gone. Obviously. Nearly chewed through my bottom lip, too."

He stuck it out almost petulantly, white bands of scar tissue criss-crossing the pink flesh.

"I'm sorry. I really am." I couldn't think of anything else to say.

"I wouldn't have left you in there. Is that how you treat all your friends?"

"Let's not do this."

He chuckled mirthlessly. "Just winding you up. I don't care about any of that. I don't care about much at all, nowadays." He stretched out his fingers, popping them one by one. "It was good to hear your version, though. Good to confirm things."

"Confirm what?" My face felt hot.

David's eyebrows rose. He looked almost mischievous. "Nobody mentioned the room. Afterwards."

"That's true."

"Feels like that should have come up in the official story. Feels like an important detail to miss out. Doesn't it?"

"It was real. If that's what you're getting at."

He leaned in. I noticed the smell, then. Like petrol, or cat piss.

"They found me on the landing. Think about it."

"Honestly? I'm stumped. Look, my bus will be here in a—"

"It let me out, Evan. It was *done* with me."

I stopped. Bile rose in my throat. "Done?"

David chuckled again. He was fiddling with his cup, pressing dirty half-moons into the Styrofoam, over and over, and it sunk in that I didn't know the man sitting across from me in the slightest. That I had known the boy he had been meant precisely nothing.

"Come on, Evan. You *know*."

I shook my head.

"Some nights," he murmured, "I wake up, and I can *almost* remember. Whatever was in there with me. With us. And I know you've had those nights too. Just a little"—he mimed a string being pulled from his ear—"tugging. At your brain. Making you wonder about all kinds of things. We could still figure it out."

"It's gone." I said. "Whatever it was. Along with the house. It's all gone."

For a brief flash, he looked almost mournful. "No, Evan. Don't you get it? It's *in us*. Right now."

Silence fell between us again. Needles of rain threw themselves against the glass.

"I saw you come in," he said, at last. "You could've left. Pretended not to see me, like everyone else in this town. Why didn't you?"

"Same reason you haven't throttled me, I suppose."

At that he barked a laugh. "All that rubbish. You shouldn't believe everything you read. No, I'll tell you why you stayed. You want me to say everything turned out alright in the end. Guess what? It didn't."

A craze of red light smeared the panes as the replacement bus wheezed up the street.

In a voice barely above a whisper, he asked me:

"Do you really think you got out without a scratch?"

"I—I need to go," I managed to force out, scraping the chair across the floor as I stood. "Good seeing you."

He gave me a look as if to say *was it, really*? But before he could speak again, I was gone.

That night, I got back to find my family asleep, the house silent and still. I turned on my laptop and searched for David online, as I had done so many times before over the years. I don't know what I wanted to find, but I got only the same old lurid headlines, the same spurious theories on true crime blogs. Any evidence connected to David as a young adult and the events that horrified the county all those years ago were patchy, riddled with gaps that you couldn't help but fill with details of your own invention. There'd been enough to put him away for a while, sure, but no longer than that.

It was done with me.

But I wasn't like him. It was like radiation, I told myself. I'd been exposed less, and so our lives had diverged. Rationalizations. Excuses.

My head hurt. I slipped into bed as quietly as I could and stared at the ceiling until, an aeon later, I plunged into a greater darkness than the one that surrounded me.

I thrashed awake in the early hours of the morning, my ribs crushing my lungs. My wife held me as I shook, shedding that caul of nightmares that clung to me no matter where I went or what I did.

"What is it?" she asked, as she'd asked so many times before. "What's wrong?"

At that moment I wish I could've spoken of an awful dream, a dream that felt real. A dream of a house that no longer existed, one with walls freshly daubed in the sour shades of viscera. A dream of windowless, crooked vaults, each lit by a single dim bulb dimming further still, each sealed by a slowly closing door. A dream of a game that was waiting to be finished, a secret waiting to be taken outside and shared with an unsuspecting world.

But I could say no such thing. For truthfully, I could not remember.

THE RITUAL OF THE LABYRINTH

ESMÉE DE HEER

IF YOU DO NOT ALREADY HAVE a labyrinth, make your own. Choose whatever materials you have at hand and try to be creative with everything you are missing. You can write down your ideas or simply imagine them. There is no need to plan it all out ahead of time. It will be better not to.

The next step is shaping your labyrinth. Work from the inside out and change direction halfway through to make sure you do not remember the path. Unlike a maze, a labyrinth has no dead ends. It consists of one path that will first confuse and ultimately calm you. The walls can be straight or crooked as long as the road remains long and winding. Do not add any flourishes. You will regret this later.

Now that the groundwork is done, imagine the walls rising. Close your eyes and see how they grow tall and reach up to the sky. The ideal height is different for everyone but what matters is that you cannot see across the walls in any way. They need to tower above you and obstruct your view. Now open your eyes and realize you have left your room behind. Gaze upon your labyrinth and step inside.

The sounds of the world dissipate once you are inside. Let your ears adjust to the quiet before going any further. You were not asked to imagine an entrance hall, but did so nonetheless. You thought up objects and decorations, but none of them are here. You will not be allowed to make up for this mistake.

Try to focus on your chosen materials. The decision to use bamboo groves was a strange one and will have its own set of unique consequences. The stalks are long, obscuring the sun and creating strange shadows behind you. They bristle in the wind, making it impossible to hear all the things that fall in step behind you. There is nothing you can do to change this now and this will mark your journey. Let your fingers graze over the textured shoots and fall in love with all the different shades of green. Close your eyes and allow the other senses to take over. Smell the rain hanging in the sky, the crisp air bright in your lungs. Pay particular attention to taste. The hints on your tongue must be floral and sweet, and only then are you allowed to proceed. Condemn the hint of resentment at the back of your throat. Swallow those bitter thoughts and be grateful you were not forced to turn back.

A cold wind rises up behind you, pushing you further into the labyrinth. You dawdle and waste time you do not have. The sun will leave you in the dark if you do not move quickly.

Finally you are moving, finding your way through the labyrinth. Once you turn the corner, open your mouth and start singing. The quality of your voice is unimportant, as long as it is loud and overpowering. Sing about all the ways in which you feel lost and do not stop, not even when the words no longer make sense. Combat the wind with your sound and drown out all the noises that are outside of you. Do not falter, there is no time to stop. Keep going, swing your arms and stomp your feet. Be loud and raucous. It is the only way to keep the danger at the heart of the labyrinth at bay. Now pick up the pace. You are close, but so are they.

Walking a labyrinth is nothing more than following a single path to its inevitable end. You look for a way out but there are no corners to cut, no tricks to get you out of its grasp. It is foolish to think you can outsmart the labyrinth and yet you keep trying. All it does is slow you down and now the shadows are encroaching. The remaining specks of light vanish as night falls and while you seem to understand that you are not safe, you are not in awe. Revere every step you are allowed to take. Be humbled by how far you are permitted to go. Look around and try to comprehend the beauty that confines you, the wonder no one else gets to see. Soon it will be time to stop. Your voice is breaking and they are catching up. Hooves clatter against the stones, breath huffing. By now you must know that this labyrinth was never yours and yet you still think you might find a way out.

Only fools find the center. Somehow you have made it here. You sang all the words your voice could carry and now the statues you imagined, the fountain, even that faded orange gate, are all there. And yet the center feels empty despite your imagination. You failed once again. There is nothing here for you. So turn around and start over. Find a way out.

The walls shift as you begin to walk, your creation changing until the labyrinth has become something else. You wander through a maze made by something else, their trials now yours to overcome. In many ways you are more lost than when you started. Now you will discover if you paid enough attention. If by now you know how to move and when to sing. Remember that a maze, unlike a labyrinth, has many dead ends and only a few places where you can hide.

THE GETAWAY

STEPHANIE FELDMAN

(After M.R. James)

THE RENTAL WAS A VICTORIAN, peaked roof and wrap-around porch, gray siding and white spindle railings, all surrounded by pines. If all I could get was another house—no city hotels or museums, no touristy plazas, and certainly no airplane rides, not while cases were rising—then this would have to do. "We just need a different set of walls," Monica and I agreed when we booked it. The past year was the longest we'd been apart since we met freshman year, almost a decade before.

I calculated our reunion was low-risk—we had quarantined and tested, and if we did get sick, we probably wouldn't die. Still, I was nervous, double-checking the address, reviewing the different routes, reloading the GPS results. The app showed a grayish, fuzzy photo of the house—taken, I figured, from one of those cars with a camera on top. Compared to the listing photo, the house appeared malnourished, infirm.

That's when I saw the figure.

The person stood in the front yard, hunched over, their shoulder blades poked through their long scraggly hair. Strange that I missed it before, but they were oddly colorless—the whole image oddly color-less, like it was taken at twilight or before sunrise. I zoomed in and the image jumped to the porch swing, the black windows behind it, the big round clock beside the door. I dragged my finger on the screen, almost expecting the lawn to be empty—the figure just a glitch or my imag-ination.

But there they were. Their face remained hidden, but now I could make out their bare feet in the dirt, and the shovel they were working into the lawn.

It must be Linda, the owner. It was probably an old picture of her at work on landscaping; when I arrived, there would be Linda's garden on the little slope. I could sit there and watch the setting sun set the flowers aglow while waiting for Monica, who wouldn't arrive until dinner.

When I pulled up to the house, the only one on the street, the kitschy clock on the porch—"Vacation time!"—read 4pm. It took several trips to unload my trunk. I packed too much: a deck of cards, yarn and needles, measuring cups and flour. After a year spent alone, I was excited to do all of these things with someone else. I didn't know what to do with someone else. I was afraid Monica might not be inter-ested in games or would be bored of baking, and sitting side by side in silence might be awkward. Less awkward, though, than talking. What did I have to report? Still at the same job, though I'd grown out of it years before; still in the same apartment, with the leak and noisy upstairs neighbors; still not dating. It hadn't felt like the right time before, and it certainly didn't feel like the right time now.

I was so busy unpacking my things and counting my worries that I didn't notice at first that there was no garden at all, and no dirt patch, just a solid green slope. Maybe that photo was very old, or maybe the garden had been another pandemic project gone awry. I hadn't started any projects myself; at first, I was too stunned, and then it felt too late. I had already become the person who would endure in a stupor.

I walked across the lawn to get a closer look. The unbroken green patch was so neat and picture perfect it gave me the chills.

I opened a bottle of wine. I stacked the board games. I thought of putting a cake in the oven, but it was too early in the week to be eating cake. I thought about how much weight I had gained and how I hadn't mentioned it to Monica—I would see it on her face, though, the first time she looked at me. Linda, the owner had changed, too; there were a couple of photos of her, one with a group of women, a few with the same man, her husband, I guessed, and she was heavier than the maps-person and with shorter hair. Either the app image was very old or very recent, and she had grown out her hair—but if it was new, wouldn't I see a garden?

I didn't see anything, really, at all when I brought my wine to the porch to wait for Monica. Just the lawn, the empty street, the thicket of stretching pines. The clock on the post ticking. It was supposed to be relaxing, this view, a park that separated the house from its neighbors, but instead it just reminded me how alone I was. I had come here to be less alone, but instead it was as if I had gone into the woods, all by myself.

Monica called.

"I missed the exit," she said. "The signal is bad out here. GPS disconnected and I didn't realize for almost 20 miles."

"Are you lost?" I asked. I pictured her holding a steering wheel, walking through those trees.

"No, I got it back. Good thing I pulled over first. I would have driven off the road. That maps photo is so weird!"

I stared at the undisturbed lawn. I shivered. I wished she would walk out of the trees and be here already. "What do you mean?" I asked.

"The figure on the porch," she said. "Is it a scarecrow or something?"

Now I imagined how awful it would be if she *did* walk out of those trees, Monica in jeans and a sweater and ponytail, a cell phone in her hand, a normal person amid those strange foreign woods. Staring at me, the figure on the porch, in horror.

"Do you mean the person on the lawn? Digging?" I meant to say gardening; I said digging.

"No, it was definitely on the porch. There was a lump on the ground next to it, like a dog sleeping? I don't know, maybe it was a shadow. Usually, those photos aren't taken at night."

"How far away are you?"

"The app says an hour and a half."

I looked at the porch clock, its pastels faded, its plastic cover cracked. Like it was making fun of time and anyone who trusted it. It was after 6pm already.

"I'll start cooking," I offered.

"Yeah, don't wait for me, I'm starving. I'll hit up a drive-through. So maybe a little longer than an hour and a half. I can't wait to see you!"

We hung up. It suddenly felt dangerous on the porch, even if there was no scarecrow or shadow. If someone did come out of those woods, if someone tried to hurt me, I'd be all alone—I'd have no help or protection.

Maybe it was safer to be alone. That's what they'd been telling us all this time.

I went inside, locked the door, locked the windows, locked the back door. Monica wanted the room at the back of the house, with the little terrace; I had agreed to take the bedroom at the front of the house, with the attached bathroom. I didn't have a preference. At some point, everything had seemed so beyond my control I had to stop caring.

I refilled my wine glass and went upstairs to unpack my clothes. Folding them neatly in the drawers, arranging my little tubes of eye creams and big tubes of hand cream in a row on top. Far tidier than I kept my things at home.

After 45 minutes, Monica sent me a photo. It seemed like it was from a different time, a better time; a better life. There was a bowl of glistening mussel shells and a tin cup with French fries. Behind it, a wine glass and a little standing card with the restaurant name and list of desserts. *Reminds me of Café Tino, remember??*

She had stopped for a whole dinner rather than a quick drive-through. Didn't she want to get here? Wasn't she excited to see me? Hadn't this been her idea? Or maybe it had been mine. Maybe she had only agreed reluctantly. She wasn't alone, after all—her boyfriend had moved in. She said she needed a break from him, but maybe she just didn't want me to feel bad.

I searched the restaurant name and put it into the map, along with the house address, to see how far away she was. Two and a half hours, it said. That couldn't be right. How had she gotten farther away? Maybe she had the wrong address, or maybe I had put the wrong address in. I tapped to check and the maps image came up. There was the dark little house on the dark empty street—almost too dark to see. Monica was right—the photo had changed. I turned my screen brightness all the way up.

The lawn was empty—no bony person digging.

I zoomed in, my heart pounding. Monica had said there was a

figure on the porch, something as spindly as a scarecrow—something, I feared, with long scraggly hair. Something that could have come from the woods or been made from the woods. But there was nothing. Nothing there. And somehow that was worse.

I zoomed in further, to the clock face, pixelated but with enough weight to suggest the time. I was curious, still, about what unusual time of day such a photo had been taken. Nearly eight—later than it was now, almost 7:30. And then I saw something beside the clock.

The window was open.

I knew, immediately, that it was true—I was shivering, the night air reaching through the house, all the way to where I hid on the second floor.

I was used to being alone, but this was different. This was worse. Why had Monica done this? Why couldn't she have left earlier, paid attention to the highway signs, driven through her hunger? She was my best friend, but I wasn't her best friend. I wasn't anyone's friend, not anymore, just a face on a screen people felt obligated to load.

I ran down the stairs. And there, the window by the door, the one I had locked—it was open.

I spun around, prepared to see that creature, bony and barefoot, with long hair and no face. All I saw was the house, another set of four walls, that I had decorated with my belongings, as if the objects that occupied my time were offerings.

I should leave. I should go out to the car and drive. But if I did that, I'd be exposing myself. What if there were more of them in the woods?

I slammed the window shut, ran back upstairs, locked the door behind me. I checked under the bed, in the closet, in the corners. Nothing. I was alone. The house beyond the door was silent. I looked out the window. It was still and silent outside, too, and dark. So dark. Night had fallen and the only lights were from these very windows, casting a weak reach outside.

I picked up my phone. I could call Monica—tell her I needed help. Tell her to stay away—it was dangerous, here, after all.

Instead, I opened the app and entered the address. The thumbnail image was the same—shadowy house against a dark sky. I zoomed in. Nothing, no one, on the lawn. No one, nothing, on the porch. The window was closed. The clock read 7:30. The exact time it was now.

The time in the photos was moving backwards. Monica had seen what would happen next: the creature would open the window and crawl out onto the porch, dragging some bundle. I had seen what would happen after that: it would dig—or, rather, fill in the hole it had dug, covering that bundle. By then it would be morning.

I moved the image around with my finger, until I saw something else in the top window, a silhouette. My silhouette. Staring out into the world, from another set of walls. A set of walls I thought would offer some kind of freedom, a getaway from the inertia and solitude that had half-buried me. That I had half-buried myself with.

I couldn't see the expression on my face, but I could see the open door behind me, and the spindly figure standing there, sack in one hand and shovel in the other.

FLESH BURNS SWEETLY

SPENCER HARRINGTON

A WAGON GROANS to a stop at the end of a long row of holes that punctuate the earth with a somber ellipse. Each hole is filled with a tangled mess of bodies. Some of them are starting to sprout—wildflowers growing from the skin—others are threatening blossoms. The flowers would be pretty if they didn't grow from flesh and blood.

Two gardeners dismount and meet at the wagon's back hatch. Down it swings with a rusty squeal. In the bed lie messy stacks of bodies. The smaller gardener, the fragile one, climbs into the wagon. Her mother called her Mabel. Over the uneven flooring of knees, elbows, stomachs, and asses, she stumbles, looking for loose change and leftover jewelry. When she's done, she slides the body to the end of the cart so that he—the strong one, the mulish one—can carry them away and dump them in the pits. His father called him many names, but the kindest was Wyatt.

Mabel slides the last body to the end of the cart and steps down. Today's haul: $3.47, a pearl necklace, and a pair of glasses (broken, she crushed them). Wyatt throws the body over his shoulder, then into the pits. Dust splashes up then dissipates. "The sun is getting low," he says, and it is. The sky is flushed like it's had too much to drink. "We should get them lit."

Oil is expensive, moonshine is not, especially the kind so motivated to burn. One by one, she soaks the piles—dead skin glistens, slack jaws collect booze—and tosses the empty bottles into the cart. *Clink, crack, shatter*. He follows behind her, striking matches and tossing them away. Like an arsenious game of dominoes, bodies catch fire one after the other. Great spires of flame dash into the sky. Embers glitter atop smoke and ash.

Mabel has gotten used to the corpses, their gaunt faces and bloated bodies. She's gotten used to the flowers, their pollen, noxious and sweet, their petals, elegant and alluring. What she hasn't gotten used to is the burning, the smell of charcoal as skin melts, of sulfur as hair is scorched. The bubbling of fat, the popping of muscles. She hasn't gotten used to the screaming. It's the flowers, she knows. A million entitled plants calling for mercy. A chorus of whistling cries. But the way they layer, the way they come like a sudden rush of rain, the way they clang through the pipes of her ears and travel to her heart and press down, down, down, leaves her standing outside a house-fire. She hasn't gotten used to the burning, but she fears she soon will. Each time it gets easier. Eventually, her stomach will harden and stop rolling at the sight of human kindling. Flesh will burn sweetly, and she will savor the taste.

The final pile ignites. The hairs on her arms curl. She turns and flees, heading to the cart to set up camp. Wyatt does not follow. For a moment, he stands at the edge of the pit, hands up, palms catching heat. There he stands as if at the height of relaxation. After a deep breath, he joins her.

Night passes slowly. The canvas of their tent dances orange and red as fires burn. Mabel wakes often, as she usually does. Each time, the colors cool. By sunrise, the bodies have been reduced to ash and the air smells of dew. In the shy colors of morning, they pack and leave.

The cart shakes as they travel across unkept trails, making it difficult for Mabel to catch up on lost sleep. By noon, they descend from the hills, onto Drescher's Landing. The next stop on their grand tour. Light seeps through platinum clouds and pours over the growing city. Rain fell recently and the roads leading in are muddy. The rough rock of the cart smooths into a gentle sway. Between this and the sloshing beneath the wheels, Mabel is finally lulled to sleep.

For a moment, she is in bliss, but by the voice of a drunk, she is forced awake. "You got any of that moonshine?" asks a disorganized man. He says moonshine as if it's two words. Their cart rolls steadily down Main Street and the man hobbles alongside them. Over and over he asks, over and over, Wyatt refuses. "Please, I'll pay top dollar. Can't you spare a bottle? Anything, just a taste. Don't hog the good stuff. Share. Please…?"

Outside the sheriff's, they stop. The drunk, deterred by men in uniform, retreats to the bar. Wyatt, thinking she is asleep, nudges Mabel awake. She groans as she lifts her head with a stiff neck. From the cart, she falls to her feet. Wyatt holds the door open, and they head inside. The room smells of sweat, mold, and iron. Daylight falls through the glass and grime and struggles to illuminate the room. Candles stand in a mess of melted wax. It is not long before they are greeted. They have been through this town many times, but still, they are only referred to as "gardeners." It is hard to call by name the person who turned your mother, your lover, your children, to ash.

After a moment of polite conversation (*how's the family? The town? The weather?*), they are taken outside, behind the building, to the old shack with the splintered door and concave roof. The door wobbles as it's opened. Inside, they find flies, bodies, flowers, but hardly enough of each.

"Where are the rest of 'em?" Wyatt asks.

"This is it," says the officer.

"It's hardly a cart full. Last we were here we took four trips."

"People aren't gettin' sick anymore. It's dyin' out."

"What about Oxtail? Or New Lafayette?" Mabel says.

"I hear it's dying out there, too. Looks like you two might be free," he laughs and pats Wyatt on the shoulder. "Here, we put a little extra in there as a thank you. We know this is tough. But hey, now you can find work that's a little more… agreeable." He hands them their money and walks inside.

Mabel and Wyatt tie their masks, don their gloves, and slip their smocks over their clothes. Together, they stock the cart. Flowers weep pollen as they carry bodies away, staining their clothes around the shoulders and at the palms of their gloves. Quickly, the cart is filled. Slowly, they leave. Wyatt holds the reins loosely. His stare is unmoving and empty. Mabel, next to him, is bouncing her legs, her boots tapping against the wood of the cart and mixing with the *clip-clop* of hooves to produce a splendid rhythm. It's cloudy outside, but never has the sun felt so golden against her cheeks. Never have the pines smelled so fresh, never have the hills produced such a heavenly view of the valley, the city, the far-off mountains. In her glee, she asks Wyatt, "What are you going to do after this?"

A moment passes, he does not speak.

"I might stay in Drescher's," she continues. "I have family there, and the city has always excited me. Maybe I'll be an actress. I've always loved the theatre, not that we went often, it was too expensive. Or maybe I'll become a writer, or a painter, or—"

"I don't know what I'm gonna do without this," he says. The words fall from his mouth like the first drops of rain. "This is it. This is all I have."

"You can stay with me in Drescher's, at least for a little while. I'm sure my aunt won't mind. She's a… peculiar sort of person, but very kind. She won't mind."

"We've never done anything else, Mabel. And who is going to hire the people that burned their families?"

Wyatt's words are heavy. Mabel watches the trees and the clouds behind them. "Don't be ridiculous," she says. "Stay in Drescher's. My family owns a lumberyard, you could work there. It might be nice for you to settle somewhere."

Mabel's words wash over Wyatt, but they do not clean. At the dirt, he stares as they ride. Hands loose, shoulders slumped, eyes oppressed by thick eyebrows.

At the pits, they stop. Mabel jumps from her seat, floating to the ground like a feather. Wyatt plummets. Through pockets, she rummages ($1.25, belt buckle, pocket watch) and sends bodies away. For a moment, after it's emptied, she lays in the back of the cart and admires the cotton sky above her before grabbing the moonshine and serving their last drink. Wyatt approaches the pit, matchbox in hand, but he does not strike a match.

From the wagon, Mabel watches over her shoulder. Wyatt kneels at the edge of the pit as if brought to his knees by grief. With a gloved hand, he cradles the bulb of a flower, holds the stem between his fingers, prods the thorns with his thumb. This is all he has. Everything else was taken, overgrown, and burned. He has gotten used to the bodies, their smell, their sound as they burn. He has gotten used to the heat of the flame, the dance of the flowers in the wind. This is all he has, there could be nothing else. There is beauty in the burning, in the colors of fire against the canvas of their tent, in the dewdrop and ash of morning, in the wagon rides through the hills, trees, and valleys. He has found beauty that he cannot abandon. Wyatt looks at the flower cradled in his hand. There is beauty here. He looks back at the cart, at the glistening bottles of moonshine not yet emptied. He looks at Mable. There is beauty beside him.

He strikes a match, flames sprout, and he returns. One hand holds the matches as he walks. The other moves discreetly into his pocket. Wyatt mounts the cart, takes the reins, and asks, "How about a drink? To celebrate," and smiles.

They find themselves in Drescher's Landing, at the pub, late at night. The band is playing ragtime, light and airy. People dance about, laughing and singing or yelling over poker (*cheater! Get him out of here!*). The bar is wet from spilled drinks (Mabel) and cluttered with shot glasses (also Mabel). Musically, she slurs nonsense, her eyes half-closed. Wyatt stands beside her as she sways, observing the room. In his hand, he holds a drink. Something simple, something strong. Mabel falls, and Wyatt, busy watching a drunken man stumble outside, is too slow to catch her.

A woman helps Mabel up, holding her hand. As Mabel talks, bashfully, about how she's normally not a klutz, the woman smiles and laughs. Wyatt sneaks off as they flirt.

Outside, the night air is cold, and fog hovers over porch lamps and streetlights. On the stoop sits a disorganized man. He smells more strongly of liquor than the bar. "Are you still lookin' for some of that moonshine?" Wyatt asks. He says moonshine as if it's two words.

❧

Wrapped in a woman's arms, Mabel wakes to a knock on the door. She dresses poorly. All she wears is not hers. She pulls open the door to find Wyatt standing behind it. Together, they walk out to the street. It's noon, the sun is high overhead and burning. She casts shade over her eyes with a hand. "There," Wyatt says, pointing out a body folded in the dirt and consumed by flowers. A crowd stands around it, murmuring. *"He was fine yesterday. How could this happen? And so quickly? Was he ever coughing up pollen? I thought the liquor would get him before the flowers."*

To the hills, they ride once more. Mabel's throat is dry, either from dread or stale drunkenness. She sucks on her tongue to fight her discomfort. Her fingers poke, pull, and scratch at each other as they ride. Whisky sweats irritate her skin, the shirt she wears is wet beneath the arms, greasy hair is tied in loose braids. Beneath her ribs, her heart pounds away. For a night, she believed it was over. How foolish. By a shepherd's hook, she was pulled off stage before she could bow and say goodnight, before the audience could cheer, applaud, and throw flowers. Wyatt beside her, she cannot be certain (the cart speaks loudly as it shakes), is humming.

Masks on, gloves on, they roll the body into the ditch. Wyatt has never seemed lighter on his feet. Mabel grabs a bottle of shine, uncorks it—*pop!*—and pours. *Glug, glug, glug,* goes the liquor. Queerly, it smells sweet. The harshness of the alcohol is chased by the scent of nectar.

Into the bottle, she peers. At the bottom sit fuzzy clumps of yellow, petals, and thorns. It smells of spring and pollen.

A match is struck, tossed away. Mabel flinches as the body erupts in large, wild flames. The heat licks at her face like a dog, the flowers whistle and scream. She looks at the bottle, at the petals within. She looks at Wyatt, at the smile he wears. She looks at the body as it burns, as skin sizzles, as fat melts, as hair goes up in smoke. She is unable to smell the char, the sulphur. All she smells is sweet.

THE MACABRE READER

LYSETTE STEVENSON

NEIGHBOR GEORGE BY VICTORIA NELSON. Cover sculpture "Horus at Edfu" by Alexander Blumenau. Strange Attractor Press, 2021.

Victoria Nelson revisits her time living in the bohemian enclave of Marin county in northern California, where, under the veneer of leftist utopianism, there lies a supernatural world upending all sense of safety and reality. Nelson amusingly uses an avian theme throughout the work and the owls are certainly not what they seem.

After settling into what appears to be a cozy town filled with quirky residents, Dovey, a twenty-one-year-old English student, is house sitting for her aunt and uncle over the summer. Dovey is disturbed by frequent news of headless bodies washing up on the shores of nearby beaches. Events that the local residents seem to brush off as inconsequential. As she drives her uncle's prized Bel Air up the winding, fog-shrouded ocean road to their remote cottage, she is haunted by the mystery surrounding her mother's death.

This lonely young woman navigates the tension between her self-determination and the eccentric local writers and artists prodding into her life. When the enigmatic neighbor George shows up, the novel gears into predator stalking prey, while otherworldly forces seek to nest in this secluded region. Nelson plays Hitchcockian twists and turns that begs to be adapted to screen. Something she has hinted could be in the works so I implore you to enjoy this sublimely written weird novel before seeing it come to life on film.

～

THE BLONDE HOUND AND OTHER STRANGE OCCURRENCES by Evan Pacewicz. Cover art by Matthew Jaffe. Swampland Press, 2022.

Set in the rainy Pacific Northwest, *The Blonde Hound* starts as a noir journey through the mind of a severe alcoholic, when he is picked up by his mother and sister from rehab to attend his father's funeral. After a heated argument he abandons them to find his own way to his family's rural homestead. Overlaid are historical accounts from the frontier, foreboding that the land his family lived on was cursed. That the devilish art his father was famous for might not have been painted from his imagination. What ensues grows from gritty to fiendish to slavishly gory as the rising cosmic horror shatters all sense of reality.

Following the novella are four grand guignols, serving as palate cleansers from the intensity of the titular story. An uncle is waylaid picking up his nephew by two menacing hitchhikers he carries in the back of the cab. A father finds his son with an unfamiliar friend on the playground and comes home with a sickness. A murderer scrambles towards a light in the woods that leads him to a demise worse than death, and a delightfully lurid correspondence between two antiquarians and a necromancer's fetish.

This is Los Angeles based writer Evan Pacewicz's second collection after his debut, *The Rats in the House*, a vibrant EC comics meets Twilight Zone inspired collection of ghastly frights.

～

THE GARDEN AT 19 by Edgar Jepson. First published in 1910. This edition Midnight House, 2002, with cover art by the prolific Allen Koszowski.

A young and upcoming London lawyer purchases a house on a largely unoccupied street. The realtor cites strange happenings driving the other residents away. Save for the next-door neighbour, an older well-travelled and curmudgeonly scholar, and his young niece. As the lawyer takes a romantic interest in the niece he also observes unusual comings and goings from her house. A cast of equally odd characters perform occult rituals in the back garden during phases of the moon. To protect her from peril, the lawyer sets out to thwart the occultists from summoning their final rite.

The character of the niece, in particular for the time, is refreshingly well developed for the first three quarters of the book before, in my opinion, disappointingly taking on the role of the damsel in distress. I still enjoyed the whole of it, nonetheless. Pulpy and fast-paced, with a great deal of enticing atmosphere. It makes a charming addition to the pantheon of weird tales.

Edgar Jepson was a prolific writer and a lifelong friend of Arthur Machen. Though not known to be a member of the Hermetic Order of the Golden Dawn, Jepson was well versed enough to lend a certain amount of credibility to his descriptions of esoteric lore, so much so, it was highly favoured by occultist Aleister Crowley.

~

A BEAM OF LIGHT IN THE DEEP FOREST by Édouard Schuré translated from French by Sam Kunkel. Published by First to Knock, 2021.

This is a collection of newly translated mystical texts by 19th century French author and occultist, Édouard Schuré. Going against the popular literary trends of naturalism and decadence in his time, Schuré's heavily macabre and direct prose poetry is spirited and grows richer with every reading.

The longest piece, "The Angel and the Sphinx," is an allegorical tale of sword and sorcery that takes you through the haunted mountains of

Germany's Black Forest. Set in the 16th century a young knight, determined to break a family curse, seeks to forge his own destiny. After consulting a magician and being given several magical objects to aid in his quest, he sets out to atone for the misdeeds of his bloodline. His journey is perilous, chased by all manner of phantom, chimera and ghoul through the wild and shadowy forests as he reclaims his dilapidated castle. Staving off encounters with a terrible femme fatale sorceress and guided by the angelic vision of his deceased mother. His quest for the Invisible Bride takes him into the abyss.

Filling out the collection are two shorter pieces that dovetail with "The Angel and the Sphinx." As well as excerpts from intimate correspondences with poet Stéphane Mallarmé, philosopher Friedrich Nietzsche and composer Richard Wagner; showing a mutual respect and admiration among these visionary artists. A fascinating scholarly exploration into a neglected figure of the fin de siècle.

～

OLD FLOATING CLOUD: TWO NOVELLAS by Can Xue. Cover art by Stanislaw Witkiewicz. Northwestern University Press, 1991.

The first novella, "Yellow Mud Street,: is a Kafkaesque vision of a factory village, where the residents live in horrid squalor but are placated by bureaucrat promises that improvements are soon on their way. Instead residents struggle to cope with sewers overflowing the streets, while mold rots their rooftops. Every detail within the lives of the villagers is beastly. The only flora is poisonous. The heat is punishing and the rain is ashen sweat. Giant bats inhabit every attic. Spiders, beetles and centipedes infest every crevasse, while it grows more surreal with lines like "Yesterday a dead tree in the park grew human hair..." The succeeding novella, "Old Floating Cloud," uses similar backdrops and elements while focusing on the psychological aftermath of a cheating husband and the deterioration of their family.

Can Xue's sense of pathos for her characters surviving against all odds makes her storytelling all the wilder and more original. With a narrative style intentionally difficult to distinguish one character from another, she produces a fever dream-like effect. Her comedic observations and deadpan delivery of the villagers spying and gossiping while carrying out their tasks and rituals, disarms you from their surrounding grotesquery.

Can Xue jokes that her own "unreadability" is what has helped her slip past the Chinese censors all of these years. With literary influences like Bruno Schultz and Borges combined with the experience of growing up under persecution during the Maoist regime; Can Xue creates mind bending narratives contrasting absurdity and horror that are an experience unlike any other.

~

THERAPEUTIC TALES by R. Ostermeier. Cover art by printmaker J. M. Walsh. Broodcomb Press, 2022.

Each book by Broodcomb, ten books and counting, is a further glimpse into the strange psychogeography of a peninsular region where the veil is always thin. A place both beguiling and frightening.

The seven stories in *Therapeutic Tales* are recorded by the new resident counsellor that serves the region's Peninsula. The counsellor walks the line between voyeur and psychopomp with their clients. A child is rendered mute after being found in a ring of yew trees. A patient is dangerously obsessed with finding hidden messages on dust jackets. A recon worker is haunted by feral cats that follow the bidding of something in the woods. Navigating shadow work, pagan traditions, experimental therapeutics, and the uncanny valley. Weirdness and technology each interplay in these tales as the counsellor begins to understand the games of hide and seek the peninsula plays.

It is fitting that this mysterious publisher resides in Cornwall county. An area steeped in dark lore, from its extensive witch trials in the 16th century to how it's considered a pilgrimage site for practitioners of witchcraft today. The writing for Broodcomb is superb and each book is a further glimpse into this queer and wayward region. With small print runs in hardcover and paperback only available from the publishing house, these books sell out quickly. While I highly recommend anything by Broodcomb, in the words of the publisher themselves, "It might not be for you."

∾

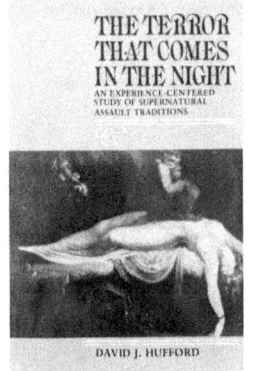

THE TERROR THAT COMES IN THE NIGHT: AN EXPERIENCE-CENTERED STUDY OF SUPERNATURAL ASSAULT TRADITIONS by David J. Hufford. University of Pennsylvania Press,1982.

What is now clinically described as 'sleep paralysis' has been documented throughout the world as far back as 906 AD as encounters with witches, devils, or ghosts. A person experiencing sleep paralysis feels they are awake, unable to speak or move their body, and frequently witnesses an apparition causing a state of heightened fear.

This book is now considered a classic and foundational text among ethnographic and sleep research. Hufford found that people were generally reluctant to share these experiences, partly out of shame of being ridiculed. His curiosity and empathy came from having had sleep paralysis himself, and he conducted interviews throughout the 1970's with a wide demographic of people. It was during his studies in Newfoundland that he discovered the term "Old Hag" was commonly used to describe the phenomenon. With a rigorous method of objective analysis he differentiates the history of nightmare phenomena; separating sleep paralysis from night terrors and hallucinations, and cataloging the widest reaches of its supernatural potential.

I had a history with sleep paralysis before I had ever heard of the term. Culminating in one of the most frightening incidents of my life: the sight of a seven-foot-tall dripping wet 'Hag' at the foot of my bed while I lay there frozen and silently screaming. Reading this book induced that same sense of engulfing terror that at any moment the Night Hag would return.

≈

THE OTHER ONE by Catherine Turney. Also published as *Possession*. Cover art by Bob Hilbert. Dell pocketbook,1952.

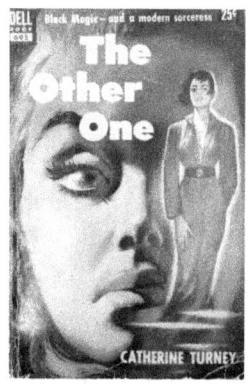

The Other One, is an entertaining occult pulp thriller, mixing references to the 1929 non-fiction book *Witches Still Live* by Theda Kenyon and nods to Arthur Machen's *The Great God Pan*. A cinematic cast of California socialites, pre-hippie cultists, and moments of shocking violence.

This 1950's California gothic is set in the quiet beachside village of Carmel on the peninsula of Monterey. The narrator, Kayt, leaves Los Angeles for Carmel after receiving a worrisome letter from her pregnant sister. After arriving, her sister has a seizure and miscarries. When she wakes up she claims to be her husband's first wife, who had died by suicide six years previously. Is it black magic or is her sister Miranda playing a cruel trick? Taking on the role of an amateur detective she investigates the former wife's background and uncovers an alleged devil worshiping cult in the hills of Monterey. Believing her sister to be possessed by the spirit of his former wife, Kayt is determined to bring Miranda back before it's too late.

Catherine Turney was one of the first female contract writers for Warner Studios. She also wrote the screenplay for the black & white 1957 film adaptation of *The Other One* entitled *Back from the Dead*, a film noir horror take on the novel starring Peggy Castle and Marsha Hunt.

CONTRIBUTORS

Barbara A. Barnett is a Philadelphia-area writer, musician, orchestra librarian, Odyssey Writing Workshop graduate, coffee addict, wine lover, and all-around geek. Her short fiction has appeared in publications such as *Lady Churchill's Rosebud Wristlet, Beneath Ceaseless Skies, Vastarien, Black Static*, and *In Somnio: A Collection of Modern Gothic Horror*. You can find her online at babarnett.com.

Eliane Boey is a Chinese Singaporean writer, with speculative stories in *Clarkesworld*, the *Penn Review*, and others. Eliane is the author of *Signal\Tracer* and *Carrier*, two novellas in a book forthcoming with Dark Matter INK in September 2023. She can be found on Twitter @elianeboey, and infrequently on Instagram @author.eliane

Winner of the Rheidol New Welsh Writing Award 2022, **Tim Cooke** is a teacher, writer and creative writing PhD student. His journalistic and critical work has been published by the *Guardian, Little White Lies, The Quietus, 3:AM Magazine, the New Welsh Review* and *Ernest Journal*. His creative work has appeared in various literary journals and magazines, including the *New Welsh Reader, The Shadow Booth, Black Static* and *Hinterland Magazine*, among others. Tim's debut collection of short stories, *Where We Live*, was released by Demain Publishing in November 2020, and he's currently working on a collection of essays to be published by *New Welsh Rarebyte*. He recently received Swansea University's James Callaghan Scholarship Prize for his research.

Esmée de Heer is a writer from Rotterdam. She works in archiving and hosts Bored to Death book club. Her work has been published in *Bear Creek Gazette* and *ergot*. You can follow her on Instagram @boredtodeathbookclub

Stephanie Feldman is the author of the novels *Saturnalia* and *The Angel of Losses*, a Barnes & Noble Discover Great New Writers selection, winner of the Crawford Fantasy Award, and finalist for the Mythopoeic Award. She is co-editor of the multi-genre anthology *Who Will Speak for America?* and her stories and essays have appeared in *Asimov's Science Fiction, Catapult Magazine, Flash Fiction Online, The Magazine of Fantasy & Science Fiction, The Sunday Morning Transport, Uncharted*, and more.

Nelly Geraldine García-Rosas was born and raised in Mexico but emigrated to the U.S. several years ago. She is a graduate of the Clarion West class of 2019. Her short fiction has appeared or is forth-coming in *Lightspeed, Nightmare, Strange Horizons*, the World Fantasy Award-winning anthology *She Walks in Shadows*, and elsewhere. She can be found online at nellygeraldine.com and on Twitter as @kitsune_ng.

Alexander Glass lives on the weird outskirts of London, England. An ex-human rights lawyer, he returned to writing in 2020 after a long period in the wilderness. His stories have been published in *The Magazine of Fantasy & Science Fiction, Asimov's, Interzone, The Third Alternative, Black Static*, and others. "The Healers" had been sitting around for a while, waiting to be written, but only took its proper shape when the ghost of Jack London wandered past.

Orrin Grey is a skeleton who likes monsters as well as the author of several spooky books. His stories of ghosts, monsters, and sometimes the ghosts of monsters can be found in dozens of anthologies, including Ellen Datlow's *Best Horror of the Year*. He resides in the suburbs of Kansas City and watches lots of scary movies. You can visit him online at orringrey.com.

Vince Haig is an illustrator, designer, and author. You can visit Vince at his website: barquing.com

Spencer Harrington is a writer from Ann Arbor, Michigan who received a Bachelor of Arts in creative writing from Grand Valley State University. After graduating, he spent a year substitute teaching before he moved to New York to pursue his creative career. Inspired by all that is strange and different, his writing gravitates towards horror, science fiction, fantasy, and magical realism. He is currently at work on a novel, trying to make the most of things.

Alex James is a writer of short stories based in West London. You can find more of his work at alex-james.com

E.M. Linden (she/her) reads and writes speculative fiction. She lives with her partner, daughter and disreputable rescue cat and likes coffee, ghost stories, and owls. Her work has appeared or is forthcoming in *The Deadlands, Kaleidotrope, Flash Point Science Fiction*, and in anthologies from Brigids Gate Press and Quill & Crow Publishing House. She has recently completed her postgrad studies in peace and conflict, has lived and worked in the Middle East and Australia but calls Aotearoa, New Zealand home.

Steve Rasnic Tem is a past winner of the Bram Stoker, World Fantasy, and British Fantasy Awards. His novel *Ubo* (Solaris Books), a finalist for the Bram Stoker Award, is a dark science fictional tale about violence and its origins, featuring such historical viewpoint characters as Jack the Ripper, Stalin, and Heinrich Himmler. He has published over 500 short stories in his 40+ year career. Some of his best are collected in *Thanatrauma* and *Figures Unseen* from Valancourt Books, and in *The Night Doctor & Other Tales* from Macabre Ink.

More of interior artist **Sumit Roy's** work can be found at Scorpydesign.com.

Rory Say is a Canadian writer of short fiction whose work tends toward the dark, strange, and speculative. Born and raised in Victoria, BC, he is currently surviving somewhere in the Pacific Northwest. Stories of his have recently appeared in *Uncharted, On Spec, Lucent Dreaming, Short Fiction: The Visual Literary Journal*, as well as on podcasts such as *NoSleep, Tales to Terrify*, and *Nocturnal Transmissions*. Learn more by visiting his website: rorysay.com

Lysette Stevenson is a stage manager with a rural outdoor equestrian theatre company and a second generation bookseller. She lives in British Columbia.

Simon Strantzas is the author of five collections of short fiction, including *Nothing is Everything* (Undertow Publications, 2018), and editor of a number of anthologies, including *Year's Best Weird Fiction, Vol. 3.* Combined, he's been a finalist for four Shirley Jackson Awards, two British Fantasy Awards, and the World Fantasy Award. His fiction has appeared in numerous annual best-of anthologies, and in venues such as *Nightmare, The Dark,* and *Cemetery Dance.* In 2014, his edited anthology, *Aickman's Heirs,* won the Shirley Jackson Award. He lives with his wife in Toronto, Canada.

Neil Williamson's work has made him a finalist for British Science Fiction Association, British Fantasy and World Fantasy Awards. He has published two fantasy novels, two collections and over seventy short stories, including a loose sequence of dark tales about strange inheritances and bequests, of which "An Antique Puzzle Chest of Unknown Provenance" is the latest. Neil lives in Glasgow, Scotland.

Our cover artist, **Asya Yordanova**, is a freelance illustrator from Bulgaria. You can find them on Twitter @artofasya

www.ingramcontent.com/pod-product-compliance
Lightning Source LLC
Chambersburg PA
CBHW071133250626
47159CB00006B/2228

9 781988 964447